Praise for *Shadows*

"With powerful tales ranging from historical fiction to contemporary stories to sci-fi and speculative fiction, the authors gently nudge readers to appreciate the importance and efficacy of praying for souls at all times of year."
Barb Szyszkiewicz, Senior Editor, CatholicMom.com

"I might never look at Halloween the same way again! These exciting and emotive stories, representing a variety of genres, draw the reader into settings and situations that shed new light on celebrating the triduum of Allhallowtide: Hallowe'en, All Saints Day, and All Souls Day. Expect this anthology for teens to cause reflection on the afterlife and to invigorate prayer for the dearly departed. It will do the same for adults! And now I must find a recipe for those delicious-sounding soul cakes."
Cynthia T. Toney, Author,
The Bird Face series and *The Other Side of Freedom*

"Spooky and satisfying! This book is a wonderful way to teach teens about the important impact our prayers have on the holy souls in Purgatory. A valuable resource!"
Catholic Mom and Daughter Channel (YouTube)

"Maybe it is because I am past the half-century mark, or maybe just finally growing up a bit, or even because I have lost a sibling to addiction, but whatever the reason, for the last five years, the concepts of Purgatory, and praying for the dead have been more and more on my mind, on my heart, and part of my daily prayers. Because of that, this anthology touched me deeply. Each of the seven stories caused me to reflect, think and pray."
(Full review on BookReviewsAndMore.ca)
Steven R. McEvoy, BookReviewsAndMore.ca

"Even the Souls in Purgatory will agree that this book is a rare and much-needed find. Any book that inspires prayers for the faithfully departed is a winner, and this collection has seven unique stories sure to inspire any teen to practice spiritual acts of mercy."

CatholicReads.com

Shadows
Visible & Invisible

By Catholic Teen Books authors:

Leslea Wahl
Carolyn Astfalk
Corinna Turner
Antony B. Kolenc
Theresa Linden
Marie C. Keiser
T. M. Gaouette

First Edition

Cover design by T. M. Gaouette
Edited by Tressa Lindsay

The following short stories are the work of the individual authors. Their inclusion here does not imply endorsement either by Catholic Teen Books or its individual authors.

Visit CatholicTeenBooks.com for more
title and author information.

Manufactured in the United States of America

Collection Copyright © 2024 Catholic Teen Books

Library of Congress Control Number: 2024917921

ISBN-13: 979-8985348521
ISBN-10: 8985348521

DEDICATION

For Saint Nicholas of Tolentino,
patron of the holy souls in purgatory and the dying.
"He spoke of the things of heaven," wrote his
biographer St. Antonine. "Sweetly he preached the
divine word, and the words that came from his lips
fell like flames of fire. Among his hearers could be
seen the tears and heard the sighs of people detesting
their sins and repenting of their past lives."

CONTENTS

For if he were not expecting that those who had fallen
would rise again, it would have been superfluous and
foolish to pray for the dead. But if he was looking to
the splendid reward that is laid up for those who fall
asleep in godliness, it was a holy and pious thought.
Therefore he made atonement for the dead, that they
might be delivered from their sin.
(2 Maccabees 12:44-45 RSV-CE)

GRACE AND THE GRAVE ROBBER

by Leslea Wahl

Austin knocks on his grandma's front door. He shuffles back and forth in the outdoor walkway of the condo as he waits for her to answer. A breeze swirls crunchy dead leaves around his worn sneakers.

Soon, the door opens to reveal Grandma's smiling face.

"Austin! I'm so glad you're here." She stands aside for him to enter. "Did you just come from working out?"

"No. Why?" He follows her gaze to his athletic shorts and bare legs, suddenly understanding her question. Nearly all the boys at his middle school dressed like this even in this cold weather, despite the complaints from their parents.

With a little grin, she shakes her head. "Your mom said you'd be stopping by after school, so I made some brownies. Do you have time for a snack?"

Austin shrugs out of his sweatshirt and flings it across one of Grandma's living room chairs. "Absolutely." He follows her and the incredible smell around the corner to her kitchen and hoists himself onto one of the stools that line the kitchen island.

He plops a thick manila envelope with the boring non-fiction book on the counter. "Here. This is from Dad."

Grandma glances at the package. "Thanks for bringing it. Your mom thought I'd enjoy the book. Although I could have gotten it another day, saving you the trip."

He shrugs. "That's okay. Changing up the routine's always a good thing." He doesn't bother to add that he was happy for the excuse to come by. Grandma is pretty good at giving advice.

She opens the fridge and pulls out a jug of milk. Austin fiddles with the corner of the envelope as she pours two glasses.

She slides one toward him. "Something on your mind?"

He raises his eyebrows as he looks at her. How does she always know when he or his siblings are distracted about something?

He takes a swig of the cold milk and then wipes his mouth with the back of his hand, ignoring the napkin she offers him.

"I'm just trying to figure out my plans for the weekend," he explains.

"Oh, yes. The triduum of Allhallowtide."

His face scrunches. "Huh?" He shakes his head, his mop of brown hair sliding across his forehead. "No, I mean Halloween."

She flashes that knowing smile of hers. "Exactly."

He stares at her for a moment, confused, then continues talking. "I got invited to two different parties and don't know which one to go to."

Her eyes light up. "That sounds like a good problem to have. Tell me about these parties. Maybe talking about it will help you decide."

He flips his hair off his face. "Well, the church is having something for the middle school youth group, and I kinda signed up to go to it. But today, I got invited to this scary-movie party."

The timer dings and the conversation pauses as Grandma removes the brownies from the oven. She places them on the cooling rack and then turns back to Austin.

"Since you already 'kinda' signed up for the church event, wouldn't it make sense to attend that one?"

He squirms in his seat. "Yeah, but the thing is, *everyone* who is anyone is going to the movie party." He picks at the envelope again. "I don't get invited to the cool parties very often. And getting scared is what Halloween's all about, right?"

Using a spatula, Grandma cuts into the soft, chocolatey snack. "Did you know All Hallows' Eve, All Souls' Day, and All Saints' Day are related? They are actually important days in the Catholic Church and form what is known as a triduum."

His mouth waters as he watches her work. "Oh, like at Easter? With Holy Thursday, Good Friday, and Easter Sunday?"

"Yes, exactly." She opens the cupboard and pulls out

two plates.

"Wait. Are you saying Halloween is a Catholic holiday?"

She slides a large brownie onto each plate. "Indeed."

"Weird. So, you think I should go to the church event." Was there any doubt that she would have chosen that one? Maybe he should have asked someone else for advice.

She carries the plates to the table. He grabs the glasses of milk and follows her.

She slides into her chair. "Watching movies with your friends does sound like fun, but that's not what All Hallows' Eve is about."

He settles into his seat, eyeing the brownie. "So, what kinds of things did you do to celebrate Halloween? You know, back in the day?"

She smiles. "My brother Harry and I did go trick-or-treating. But my most memorable All Hallows' Eve was spent with my family on one of my dad's excursions."

Unable to wait any longer, Austin picks up his brownie. "One of his archaeological digs?" As his teeth sink into the homemade delicacy, his eyes close, savoring the treat.

"It wasn't an excavation, but he was on the job. But maybe you don't have time to hear the story right now."

Austin swallows his bite, anxious to hear more. Her stories about her archaeologist father always fascinate him. "No, please. I'd like to hear it."

"Oh, good. Because the story of the grave robber is quite interesting."

Austin's eyes widen.

1958

"Gra-ace!" Daddy calls, exasperation adding an extra syllable to my name.

"Coming!" I holler back. Even though we'll only be gone for the weekend, I have no idea what to pack. We're staying at a church, going to Mass, and attending some kind of fall festival. Wanting to be prepared, I may have overpacked. I latch up my suitcase then lug it out the door to our big family car. The Chevy is large, but the trunk is already full of all of Mama's art supplies.

Daddy takes one look at my suitcase and lets out a huge sigh. "Are you turning into your mother, having to bring everything you own?"

Mama pats his arm. "Hon, I believe that when you were persuading me to come with you this weekend, you said I could bring my painting supplies along." She reaches into the trunk and taps the brown case he always takes on his archeological assignments. "Maybe you could leave some of your items at home."

Daddy pulls her close and kisses her cheek. "You're right, darling. Your passion is just as important as mine." He lets her go and points a finger at me. "Thank goodness your journaling requires only a pencil and a pad of paper. Otherwise, we might need to get a larger car."

I give him my most mischievous grin. "Actually, I was thinking of taking up a musical instrument. Maybe the tuba?"

He playfully groans.

I wrap my arms around my suitcase and hold it against my chest. "Don't worry. This can sit on the back seat between Harry and me. It can be my desk as I write in my journal."

"It better not cross the line to my half!" Harry yells from the back seat. "I need to save room for any treasures I find."

My older brother has recently begun collecting things he finds. So far most of it has been junk, but he's always hoping to discover something valuable.

Before long, we're heading down the road, off on another family adventure.

I pull out my journal, careful not to push my suitcase too close to Harry. I don't want to get on his bad side right away. A grumpy Harry always makes for a long car ride.

I date the top of a clean page. "So, where did you say we were going?"

Daddy turns his head slightly to talk over his shoulder. "We're headed across the river to Illinois."

I write down this information. "And why are we going there?"

"A church there has some items they want me to identify. The priest invited you because this weekend is their big All Hallows' Eve celebration."

That part, I remembered—part of the reason for the larger-than-usual piece of luggage.

I jot a few notes, then close my journal and watch out the window as the barren fields blur past, ready for another adventure.

"Turn here," Mama directs as she studies the map and Daddy's handwritten directions.

Daddy slows the car and turns right onto a dirt road. I sit up, awed by the towering trees that line both sides of the road. The dark trunks and bare branches intersect, creating a web above the road, dimming the midday, overcast light even further.

"Creepy," Harry murmurs.

Mama's eyes widen in amazement. "Think how beautiful this must be in the spring and summer when you're driving through a canopy of green."

We continue down the long drive, and finally, the trees thin out enough that the tall dark spires of a church come into view.

The land to the left of the church might be pretty in the summer when it's all green and lush, but now, at the end of October, various shades of brown alternate with evergreens, which appear dark gray against the cloudy sky. Tall brown grasses are interspersed with the brown sticks—all that remain of the numerous bushes, flowerbeds with dead flowers, pathways covered in crunchy leaves, and expansive lawns with straw-colored grass. The benches, gazebo, and picnic tables, which are probably inviting in the spring, are also darkened by shadows from the spindly trees.

To the right of the church is a brick two-story building. The wooden front door swings as we open our car doors. A man in a long black cassock shuffles our way.

Daddy strides toward him and clasps his hand in

greeting. "Father O'Malley?"

"Yes, thank you so much for coming, Professor Turner."

"Call me Mac," Daddy says.

The jovial man with small, rounded glasses and a shock of white hair smiles at us. His Irish accent adds a hint of whimsy to his words like he's telling a tall tale. "I'm so glad you all could come. You will love our annual parish All Hallows' Eve celebration."

Mama smiles. "Thank you for inviting us."

The priest claps his hands. "Well, come, come. Let's get you settled. You will stay in the main house. My housekeeper, Mary, was thrilled to finally have a reason to make up some of the rooms we rarely use."

We gather our bags and follow him into the building. Mama oohs and aahs over all the dark wood, but I'm transfixed by all the life-size statues that fill the place.

Mary, the housekeeper, with a mass of gray hair piled on top of her head, appears out of nowhere and beckons us to follow her up the stairs to where we'll be staying.

She's busy chatting with Daddy and Mama, while I lag behind, staring at all the religious paintings and statues of various saints that also reside on this level.

Mary stops. Her bony hand gestures into one room. "Professor and Mrs. Turner, you can stay here."

I peek in at the large four-posted bed and the antique lamp on the nightstand.

"When I heard we'd be staying at the rectory, I was not expecting something so fancy," Mama says, reading my mind.

Mary smiles. "Oh, yes, that's what most guests say. When this place was built in the late 1800s, the church's generous benefactors, Mr. and Mrs. Dupree, insisted on furnishing the rooms. The priests thought it was inappropriate to live in such luxury, but they eventually compromised. Their rooms are very sparse."

"Dupree, the family we are here about?" Daddy asks.

Mary nods. "The one and only. I'm sure Father O'Malley is anxious to tell you all about it." Mary sharply turns and crosses the hall in two quick steps. "Your room is here, Harry, and yours there, Grace. Why don't you get settled and then come down for lunch."

As I step into my room, my breath catches. It takes all my willpower not to take a flying leap and jump onto the tall, inviting bed full of fluffy pillows. Who cares about unpacking? I just want to take in every detail, from the floral wallpaper to the red velvet curtains. This room makes me feel like a princess.

Pulling the heavy curtain aside, I peer out the window. It overlooks a garden. Most of it is clear, but a few pumpkins add a small burst of color to the palette of brown.

I am still not unpacked when Mama announces it's time to go down for lunch. I skip down the hall toward the stairs where Mama and Daddy are waiting. As I pass one of the towering statues that line the hall, something jumps out at me.

"AHH!" Harry yells.

I screech in response, my hand resting on my racing

heart.

"Harry!" Daddy scolds in that tone that makes us immediately stand at attention. "We are invited guests in Father O'Malley's home."

"Sorry," Harry says, lowering his voice. "I just couldn't resist. This place is so crazy with all these statues." His eyes light up with an idea. "Would it be okay for Grace and me to play hide-and-seek here?"

"No!" Mama and Daddy say in unison.

Harry frowns.

I try to make him feel better. "I bet there are just as many interesting places outside to play."

By the time we enter the dining room, Harry is no longer pouting. But the idea of heading outside vanishes from my mind as I take in the beautiful paintings and dark wood. This place has to be as pretty as any castle in England.

Father O'Malley sits on one side of the long table. Bowls of soup and a platter of sandwiches await us, which causes my stomach to rumble.

I wait patiently during Father O'Malley's prayer before reaching for one of the sandwiches.

As we eat, Daddy and Father O'Malley discuss the reason we are here.

"So," Daddy says in that serious professor tone of his. "Mary told us that Mr. and Mrs. Dupree were the ones who left all the fine furnishings for this rectory."

Father O'Malley glances around. "Yes, a bit extravagant, isn't it? But the space works well for holding meetings and for hosting visiting priests and other guests."

"And that is the same family you told me about?"

"Yes, yes," Father O'Malley answers. "They were a very wealthy family. As I told you on the phone, when each of the various family members passed away, some of their favorite items were placed in the family vault in a specially designed space in front of their caskets. Glass kept them safe from the elements, making the crypt a bit of a museum."

Harry and I glance at each other, our curiosity on high alert.

"Several weeks ago, our groundskeeper heard strange sounds out in the cemetery and went to explore. We found him unconscious in the crypt. The thief must have hit him on the head, knocking him out. We surmise the thief was worried about getting caught, and so he left in a hurry, taking only some of the valuables. The rest were found in a pile in the center of the crypt."

"Oh, the poor man," Mama says.

"Yes, he still hasn't regained consciousness. We are praying that he survives." We all follow Father O'Malley's lead as he makes the sign of the cross.

"What is it that you think I can help with?" Daddy asks.

"I'm not sure we'll ever recover the stolen items, but we can take care of the remaining pieces. In our records, we have the descriptions of which valuables belonged to which family member. But many of the items' descriptions are so similar that I've been unable to match the items to their descriptions. A friend told me some of the work you've done for the Church, and I thought you might be able to help."

Daddy slowly nods. "I will certainly try. It doesn't sound like the project will be too difficult."

"Wonderful." Father O'Malley looks over at Harry and me. "While your father works on that, maybe you could help us prepare for the party?"

"Sure!" we say in unison.

"First, let me tell you about our annual event. I've missed some of the traditions from my youth back in Ireland, so when I started at this parish, I decided to implement a few of them. The community has been kind to this sentimental old man and embraced my somewhat odd ideas."

Harry and I lean forward, hoping to catch every heavily accented word.

"Unlike many parishes, we celebrate every day of the Allhallowtide triduum. It begins this afternoon with families knocking on their neighbors' doors."

"To go trick-or-treating?" I ask.

His eyes twinkle behind his little round glasses. "I bet you didn't know *that* modern tradition came from a Catholic event called souling."

Harry and I look at each other and shake our heads.

"I don't know exactly when it began, but souling became a tradition when poor people visited the homes of wealthier families. They promised to pray for the souls of relatives who had passed away in exchange for a little round pastry called a soul cake."

My eyes widen. "Really?"

Father O'Malley nods. "Yes. So, each parish family now visits a neighbor and asks if they have a deceased relative they would like the Church to pray for. They bring the names to the parish in the evening for a prayer service, where we write those names in a book for our All Souls' Day Mass. Then we enjoy our party with lots of food and games."

"That's so neat," Harry says.

The elderly priest nods in agreement. "Everyone also brings food for the feast. And Mary always makes two of my favorites, barmbrack and colcannon." He closes his eyes and smiles, as if remembering their taste.

"Those sound like Irish delicacies," Mama says.

"Oh yes, barmbrack is a fruit bread with a special hidden charm inside."

"Like a king cake for Mardi Gras?" Daddy asks.

"Exactly. And don't miss the colcannon. Mary makes the best cabbage and boiled potatoes."

I'm not sure either of those sound like my cup of tea, but I'm willing to give them a try.

"How can we help you get ready?" Harry asks.

"Late in the evening, we have a large bonfire, and people enjoy putting candles in their carved containers to carry along."

"Oh," I say. "I saw the garden from my window. Do you want us to go gather the pumpkins?"

He grins. "You can get the pumpkins for decoration, but turnips are what we carve."

My face scrunches in confusion. "Turnips?"

"Oh, yes. It's another ancient tradition. You'll find a wheelbarrow full of them in the greenhouse."

I'm still trying to figure out how one goes about carving a turnip, when Harry pushes away from the table.

"No problem," Harry says. "Grace and I can get those. Do you mind if we wander around the property?"

"Of course not. Enjoy the mild afternoon."

Harry and I grab our jackets and exit the building.

I point toward the right. "I noticed the greenhouse that way."

He waves me off and starts walking in the opposite direction, to the other side of the church. "This property is huge. It's perfect for hide-and-seek."

We wander into the park, or maybe it's more of a massive garden, that I'd seen as we drove in. As we walk, I'm on the lookout for great hiding spots, but when I notice a few little houses on the far end of the property, another idea begins to take shape.

"Harry, look." I point toward the cottages. "What do you think about trying our hand at souling? It would be nice to have a name to add to the prayer book tonight."

His eyes narrow as he peers in the direction I'm pointing, then his face breaks into a smile. "Good idea. But don't think this gets you out of hide-and-seek."

Our shoes crunch through the fallen leaves as we trek to the homes. Harry stops a few times to pick up items which he shoves in his pocket: a lost hair clip, a shiny gold button, and a small empty jar.

Our initial excitement turns to discouragement when no one answers the door at either of the first two homes. But on our third attempt, the door is opened by a thin woman in a worn housedress. Her hair is pulled back, making it hard to tell how old she is. I guess she's maybe a little younger than Mama.

"Can I help you kids?" she asks.

Her sad eyes make me suddenly unsure how to explain our mission, but Harry has no such problem and tells the woman all about souling. I don't know what I expected, but it wasn't the tears that suddenly stream down her face. I glance at Harry, who's looking as shocked as I am.

The woman swipes at her tears and offers us a small smile. "Oh, this is so wonderful. Thank you. You are truly a blessing. You see, my brother passed away just last week. He was in a car accident." She begins weeping again.

Harry shuffles from one foot to the other. "We are happy to pray for his soul."

"God listens to prayers," I add, not knowing what else to say.

"Please wait." She disappears into the house. When she returns, she hands Harry two pieces of paper. The top square of paper has a name written on it. "His name is RJ."

Harry turns to leave, but an idea stops me from joining him.

"You should come join the party at the church this evening, then you can join in the prayers."

The woman's gaze flicks over our shoulders to the church behind us. "I've never been much of a church-going person."

"Well, a party is a good time to start," I add cheerfully.

"Or you could attend the All Souls' Day Mass," Harry adds.

She bites her lower lip. "I'll think about it."

After she closes the door, Harry and I start back toward the church property.

"How amazing is that? For us to find someone who really needed prayers for their loved one," Harry says as he stuffs the papers in his pocket.

"God definitely led us to the right house."

Harry nudges me with his shoulder. "Maybe if you're lucky, He'll lead you to me. You're the first seeker." Before I can answer, he sprints away.

"Fine," I sigh and sit on the cool ground on a blanket of leaves. With my eyes squeezed shut, I start counting to fifty. I try to listen to the sound of snapping branches or the sound of crisp crumbling leaves to get a sense of which direction he headed, but he's as stealthily quiet as usual.

When I'm finished counting, I peel my eyes open. I remain sitting for a moment, looking and listening for any clue as to where Harry is hiding. Nothing. With so many large trees, the hiding places are endless. I let out another sigh and push myself off the ground.

My search continues until I'm no longer in the park area but have reached the cemetery that lies behind the church. Given my father's line of work and my mother's preoccupation with anything that might be deemed artistic, I've been around my share of graveyards. The stone monuments and ornate headstones usually aren't creepy to me but are symbols of untold stories.

Forgetting about my brother, I wander through the rows, looking at the names and dates. Each headstone is unique: impressive-looking obelisks, stone angels, and benches in various shades of gray. Some are so old the stones are crumbling or are too weathered to read. While they are all fascinating, one particular structure catches my eye and draws me toward it.

In the middle of the graveyard is what looks like a little stone house. As I get closer, I notice an open doorway on the back of the structure. A web of ropes blocks my entrance. Carved into the stone at the top of the doorway is the word Dupree.

Oh! The crypt that was broken into. I step closer and peer in. The deep shadows make it hard to see much, but I can make out the rectangular holes in the wall in front of me. A shiver runs down my spine when I realize caskets must be in that wall.

"Boo!"

I jump at least a foot off the ground, my heart hammering inside my chest. I spin around and glare at Harry. Why do I keep falling for his nonsense?

He laughs. "You deserve that one. Were you ever going to come find me?"

"I got side-tracked. Look, this must be the crypt that was robbed."

He peers up at the name. "Yeah, I guess so. Hey, I saw a car pull up to the church. I think people are starting to arrive. We'd better go get those turnips."

With one last look at the Dupree crypt, I follow him toward the greenhouse.

By the time we change clothes and leave the rectory, quite a few families have arrived for the evening's festivities. As we make the short walk to the church, Daddy tells us about his afternoon and how he was able to help Father O'Malley match the items with the descriptions in the burial information.

"It wasn't difficult. I'm actually a little surprised no one tried to steal the items before. They were quite valuable. The church is raising money to purchase thicker glass so people can still admire the pieces. Too bad half the items are probably gone forever."

When we reach the sanctuary, Mama and I are both so transfixed by the gorgeous stained-glass windows that Daddy has to physically guide us to an open pew.

Father O'Malley begins the prayer service by thanking everyone for participating in the souling activity. Everyone is then invited to come forward and write the names they collected in the book of the deceased. Harry and I walk up, and since I have better penmanship, he lets me write the name from the paper, RJ Tubbs, in the book.

Father O'Malley leads us in reciting a few psalms and then a prayer for the repose of the souls written in the book.

Our family follows the rest of the congregation to the fellowship hall for the party. Harry immediately makes a beeline to the back wall where long tables overflow with all kinds of yummy-looking foods. I take a moment to check out the activity tables. Our turnips are at one station. A woman demonstrates how to carve the turnip so it will hold a candle, turning the vegetable into a little lantern. I move on to watch a blindfolded boy try to take a bite out of an apple that is dangling from a string. His friends cheer him on.

"Well, what do you think of our celebration?"

I glance up to see Father O'Malley standing next to me.

"I love it. This has been such a wonderful day."

His eyes sparkle with delight. "Well, I'm so glad you could join us. I'd like to give you this." He hands me a little doll made out of a corn husk.

"Oh! It's so sweet! Did you make this?"

"Indeed, I did." He holds up a basket full of cornhusk creations. "It's a little hobby of mine. May the doll always remind you of this special night."

"Thank you. I will treasure it always." I already know the perfect place of honor on my bedroom bookshelf.

He smiles and then turns to hand another homemade item to a little boy.

I make my way to find my family.

After we eat, play a few games, and carve our turnip lanterns, Father O'Malley announces it is time for the ceremonial walk to the bonfire. Once all the little candles are lit, we follow the elderly Irish priest in a single file out the door toward the cemetery.

The flickering lights of the candles against the

darkening night sky are so pretty as we weave through the cemetery. I can't help but think of all the people buried here who are now up in heaven, thankful for the prayers we've offered up this evening. Our parade ends at a large bonfire. We toss our turnips into the dancing flames.

Someone starts singing "Amazing Grace," and every voice joins in. Harry grins at me, and I stifle a giggle, remembering the time he convinced me the song was written about me. My gaze drops to the cornhusk cross he is holding, another of Father O'Malley's creations. I pat my pocket for my cornhusk doll, but my pocket is empty.

Oh, no! It's missing! I must have dropped it during our walk through the cemetery.

I lean toward Harry and tell him I'll be back in a few minutes, then I retrace my steps. The sky continues to darken, and the further I get from the fire, the harder it is to see, but the cream-colored doll on the dark stone path should be easy to spot. While most people are gathered around the fire, I'm not alone in the cemetery; a few folks continue their walk through the graveyard, looking at the various headstones.

I'm concentrating so much on the task at hand that I don't notice the person sitting on a bench next to the path until he speaks. I let out another little shriek, this one sounding a bit like a wounded animal.

"I'm sorry," says a deep voice. "I didn't mean to scare you."

I look at the person sitting on the bench. He's holding one of the turnip candles, which makes shadows dance across his face. In the dim light, it's hard to tell how old he is, but it would be safe to say he's somewhere between Harry's and Daddy's ages. Of course, that doesn't narrow it down much.

"Are you going to join the bonfire?" I ask.

He turns to look at the glowing fire, which highlights the side of his face. That's when I notice all the freckles that color his cheeks.

"I'm not sure," he replies. "I hoped to talk to Father O'Malley, but he seems pretty busy."

I nod. "Yeah, it's a pretty big night for him. Maybe he'll have more time tomorrow."

The corners of his mouth pull his expression into a frown.

"My family is staying at the rectory tonight. I could give him a message if you'd like," I offer.

"I'd appreciate that. You can tell him that Finley will return to work soon. And, if it's not too much to ask, my family needs help, but they are too proud to ask."

In my mind, I repeat the message so that I won't forget. "Got it."

"Are you looking for something?" he asks.

"Yeah. I lost a little cornhusk doll that Father O'Malley made for me."

"Well, since I'm unable to talk with him, I'll help you look." He pushes off the bench, and soon his long, lanky body is towering over me. His clothes are worn and tattered. He wasn't kidding about his family's need.

"Thanks. By the way, I'm Grace."

He smiles. "I'm Bobby."

We follow the path all the way back to the church without finding the doll. Disappointment wells inside me. "Oh, well. Thanks for helping me look. Maybe someone saw it and picked it up."

Bobby's head tilts to the side. "You said it was made of cornhusk?"

I nod.

"Maybe a critter picked it up. The squirrels here are notorious for gathering all kinds of things."

"Just like my brother." I look up, picturing my delicate treasure up in the branches of one of the trees.

"And I know where they like to store all their treasures." He turns and starts walking back the way we came.

I scurry after him. His long legs make it challenging to keep up. "I guess it's worth a look."

When the path splits in two, he takes the path that veers away from the bonfire and heads toward the shadowy Dupree crypt. Before we make it there, Bobby stops at a short rock wall.

He moves his candle along the top of the wall, and I see the structure used to be taller but collapsed at some point, leaving behind a mound of stones. "If you're brave enough to search, you'll find all kinds of treasures there."

It does look like a good hiding spot—for raccoons. Maybe Harry can help me look tomorrow. I turn to tell him thanks but no thanks, when something catches my eye. My doll is on the ground next to the decaying wall.

"Hey, look!" I bend to pick it up. I brush a bit of dirt off it, then turn to my companion. "Thanks!"

"Just returning the favor for relaying my message to Father O'Malley."

"I promise I won't forget. But I'd better get back to my family. It was nice to meet you."

He nods, then turns and slowly walks away. I watch him for a moment, then skip back to the bonfire before my parents start to worry about me.

The next day, I'm sitting next to Mama on the side porch as she captures the majestic church and picturesque cemetery on her canvas. I'm writing all about yesterday's adventures before I forget.

The peaceful quiet is interrupted when Fr. O'Malley, Daddy, and Harry return from their walk around the property.

Mama sets down her paintbrush when they join us. "How was your walk?"

"It was great!" Harry exclaims as he plops down next to me on the wicker bench. "I found a super cool rock, a rusty toy car, and part of a gold chain." He pulls his treasures from his pockets and lays them on the table for us to admire. Among the items he's collected over the last two days is the cornhusk cross from Father O'Malley.

"Oh! Father O'Malley, I nearly forgot," I say. "Last night, someone asked me to give you a message." I scrunch my face trying to remember Bobby's exact words. "He told me his family needed assistance."

Father O'Malley smiles. "Well, we certainly can try to help with that. But I may need a little more information to go on. There are a lot of people in our community that are in need."

"He said his name was Bobby."

Father O'Malley's brow furrows. "Hmm. . . not much to go on. Hopefully he will come by again."

"He also wanted to let you know that Finley will be returning to work soon," I say.

All color seems to drain from Father O'Malley's face, and he sinks into one of the chairs. "Someone told you that last night?"

"What's wrong?" Daddy's concerned face turns toward the elderly priest.

"Finley is our groundskeeper. The police wanted to keep his condition quiet so as not to alarm the town. I told you about him, but no one else beside the police and Mary knew his identity, not even the hospital staff. He was admitted as a John Doe. He wasn't expected to live, but right before we left for our walk, the detective called to tell me Finley opened his eyes this morning. A true miracle."

All eyes turn to me.

"Grace." Daddy's eyes narrow. "Who did you speak to?"

I picture Bobby and his shabby clothes. "I don't know. He was just a guy helping me search for the cornhusk doll I dropped."

Father O'Malley's eyes widen. "There is one other person who would know Finley was hurt. The one who injured him."

I lean back, stunned. *Bobby? Could Bobby be the grave robber? He seemed so nice.*

"Grace, do you remember what the man looked like?" Mama asks in a whisper.

I look down at the table, trying to concentrate on Bobby's features when I'm suddenly staring right at his face. I reach into the pile of items from Harry's pocket and pull out a faded photograph of a young man with a face full of freckles. "This is him." I look up at Harry. "Where'd you find a picture of Bobby?"

Harry's eyes narrow. "I didn't find it. Yesterday, that woman gave me this photo along with her brother's name. That is a picture of her brother that died, RJ."

I turn the photo over and read the handwritten words scrawled across the back. "Thank you for praying for my deceased brother, Robert James—Bobby."

Present Day

"*What?*" Austin yells, interrupting the story. "You were talking to a ghost?"

Grandma raises her shoulders in a slight shrug. "I like to think that maybe it was poor Bobby's guardian angel helping him make things right."

"Whoa!"

Grandma smiles and leans back in her chair. "We found out later that Bobby had lost his job and was so worried about making ends meet that he decided to steal the valuables from the vault and sell them. When the groundskeeper, Mr. Finley, surprised him, he threw one of the items at the elderly man, which caused him to lose his balance and fall, hitting his head on the stone.

"Bobby was scared that he'd killed the man, so he ran off with some of the treasure. He was afraid to try and sell the items, so he hid them. Eventually, the guilt got to him, and he told his sister. She convinced him to take the valuables back to the church. Before he had a chance, he died."

"Oh, geez," Austin says. "That's so sad. Did they ever find the rest of the valuables?"

Grandma grins. "As a matter of fact, they did. I remembered the hiding spot Bobby had shown me. And what do you know? The missing items were hidden in that pile of rubble."

"What happened to Bobby's sister?"

"Father O'Malley asked her to work at the church, helping Mary."

Austin leans back in his chair. "Do you think all that was uncovered because you and Harry prayed for his soul?"

"Possibly. It certainly didn't hurt. But ever since then, Halloween has held a different meaning for me. I realized how important it is to pray for those who have died because they can no longer pray for themselves."

"Man, that's an amazing story. I can't wait to tell my youth group about it."

"Does that mean you'll be spending Halloween at

church?"

Austin nods, his shaggy hair sliding over his eyes. "Souling was one of the activities listed on the flyer. I didn't know what it was. But that sounds way cooler than some dumb movie marathon. Who knows who we might be able to help?"

Grandma smiles as she reaches for another brownie. "Indeed. God works wonders through our prayers." She glances at the package Austin had brought with him. "You know, that's exactly what the book your mom sent is about, the miraculous power of prayers." She looks at her youngest grandson. "Perhaps you'd like to borrow it when I'm finished?"

Austin grins. "Yeah, I'd like that. That actually sounds really cool."

The characters in this story are featured in the short story *Grace Among Gangsters* in the CTB anthology, *Treasures: Visible & Invisible*. You can also look for them in an upcoming teen novel, *A Summer to Treasure*, by the author.

ABOUT THE AUTHOR

LESLEA WAHL is the author of the award-winning Catholic teen mysteries *The Perfect Blindside, eXtreme Blindside, Where You Lead, Into the Spotlight,* and *Charting the Course.* Leslea's journey to become an author came through a search for value-based fiction for her own children. She now not only writes for teens but also has become a reviewer of Catholic teen fiction to help other families discover faith-based books. Leslea lives in her beautiful home state of Colorado with her husband. The furry, four-legged members of her family often make cameo appearances in her novels. Leslea has always loved mysteries and hopes to encourage teens to grow in their faith through these fun adventures. For more information about her faith-filled Young Adult mysteries, please visit www.LesleaWahl.com.

2

BOGEY IN THE BELFRY

by Carolyn Astfalk

1880s

Fourteen-year-old William raced down the stairs, his shoes slapping against the wooden treads, nearly toppling his little sister Margaret. Why was she always underfoot?

"Hey!" Margaret cried, clutching the railing. "You almost knocked me over!"

William had already reached the bottom of the stairs and was grabbing his coat from the coat tree, causing it to tip precariously on two feet before gravity steadied it. "Sorry." He shoved his arms into the coat. "Tell Ma I'll be back—"

"Don't you want your cakes?" Ma emerged from the kitchen, a sack in one hand. Steam escaped through the loosely woven fabric of the sack as she pushed a loose strand of hair from her forehead, and a spicy-sweet aroma drifted lazily toward Will.

He inhaled, savoring the scent, and hurried toward Ma. He grabbed the sack tightly in his fist. He'd promised his friends Stanislaw and Zofia he'd bring the cakes; they were supposed to bring some holy cards.

"Thanks, Ma!" He turned and hustled to the door, only half-listening as she said something about her shoulder hurting and that must mean rain was coming. William didn't hang around for her full forecast.

William pounded down the porch steps and turned toward Stanislaw and Zofia's house. He tugged at his open coat and fumbled with its buttons as a breeze sent icy air over the gooseflesh on his arms and sides. An early snow wasn't unheard of in southwestern Pennsylvania in late October, but Ma's shoulder said rain, right?

He peered at the sky, where darkening clouds gathered in the west, obscuring the sunset and hastening twilight. Turning, he glanced toward home, where the eerie glow from a carved pumpkin stood stark against the quickly graying landscape. Pumping his arms to move faster, William turned the corner toward his friends' house and—

"Whoa!" Two hands reached out, bracing his shoulders, and the sack of sweet soul cakes nearly fell from his grip. "Where are you headed so fast?"

William's pounding heart steadied as he recognized Dennis, his eyes keen and sharp beneath his cap. "None of your bees-ness," he quipped, echoing little Margaret's favorite answer to nearly every question asked.

At that, his brother Dennis dropped his hands and grinned, probably imagining Margaret, arms crossed and nose in the air as she delivered her signature reply. His gaze lowered to the fragrant sack. "Oh, man. Are those

Ma's soul cakes? Can I have one?"

At seventeen, Dennis was perpetually hungry, but never more than when he came home from work, like now. He reached for the bag, but William snatched it away before its contents ended up in Dennis's belly.

"There are more at home. I'm taking these with me. Stanislaw and Zofia have never had any, and there might not be any left by the time we get back home." He shifted the bag behind him, just in case Dennis—bigger, taller, and stronger than him—got any ideas.

"You'll get some at other houses." Dennis peered around William's back, eyes on the sack.

"Ma's are the best though." Dennis couldn't argue with that. Their ma was the best baker in the neighborhood.

"All right then. I'll get my fill at home," he said, rubbing his belly.

William stepped around him with a goodbye nod, only getting a few yards before Dennis called out behind him.

"Watch out for the *púca*!" Dennis made a scary call— part howl, part laughter.

William shook off a shudder. He was far too old to be put off by the silly tales his parents had brought with them from Ireland. No blood-thirsty, shape-shifting creature would trouble him tonight. All superstitious nonsense, that's what it was. William trusted God in all things; there'd be no reason to fear this All Hallows' Eve.

Soon the sky had blackened both from sunset and the gathering storm, and William arrived at his friends' doorstep. Before he had a chance to knock, Zofia opened the door, her blonde braids tucked under a cap. She smiled at William, then called behind her for her twin brother.

Stanislaw came running from behind her, pushing Zofia through the door's threshold onto the street, then slammed the door shut behind him. "Do you have the soul cakes?" His gaze settled on William, and his features softened, looking apologetic. "Oh, *cześć*, William."

William laughed and hefted the bag of soul cakes, the tension created by Dennis's mention of the púca finally leaving him. "Greetings to you too! Ready?"

Zofia and Stanislaw gave their assent, and they set off in the direction of the Irish neighborhood, back toward William's home. He wanted to introduce his friends to souling, since they'd not heard of it before. Only the Scottish and Irish families ventured out, going door to door offering prayers or a little entertainment in exchange for a cake.

"Zofia, do you have the holy cards?" William hoped she hadn't forgotten or exaggerated her ability to get some (as she was wont to do). They could offer them in exchange for cakes too.

"Yes, in my pocket." She pulled a handful from her coat. "St. Casimir, St. Stanislaw Kostka, the Blessed Virgin, baby *Jezus*, young *Jezus* . . ." She shuffled the cards in her hands, her litany drifting off as she appeared to organize them.

William hadn't heard of any of them, aside, of course, from the Blessed Mother and Jesus. Where were St. Patrick, Sts. Brendan and Bridget? Well, she'd brought cards as she said she would, even if they were strange Polish people he'd never heard of.

Lightning flashed in the distance, lighting his friends' faces with a pallid glow as thunder rumbled behind them. Within seconds, the air felt and smelled of rain. Ma's shoulder never failed.

"Let's duck inside the church!" William shouted as rain suddenly pelted them. He tucked the sack of soul cakes under his coat in an effort to keep them warm, if not dry.

The three friends rushed up the steps of Saint Columba, and William yanked open the heavy door. They stumbled inside, rainwater dripping from their noses and chins, running off their backs. How had it gone from dry to torrential downpour so quickly?

The narthex of the cavernous church, barely warmer than the outdoors and dimly lit, would serve as their refuge, for now. Ma's admonitions to wipe his feet ringing in his head, William used the rug laid there for that purpose.

The rain pounded on the rooftop for several minutes. When it slowed, Stanislaw poked his head out the door. "It's not so bad now," he reported, "but it's still raining enough to soak us."

Zofia sat on a stiff bench. On Sundays, the elderly women with pained knees waited there while their families chatted and mingled. She withdrew the holy cards from her pocket and thumbed through them, humming softly.

William sat next to her, removed the soul cakes from

beneath his coat, and offered one to her and to Stanislaw, who sat on his opposite side. "Now you'll have to pray for me da and all the deceased members of the Cook family."

It'd been nearly five years without Da, but lately, the loss stung, sharp and fresh. William had been grasping at every memory of Da he could call to mind, scared that the wispy recollections would soon fade.

"Mmm," Stanislaw said, his eyes closed as he devoured the cake. "So good."

His sister nodded her agreement. "Delicious. Maybe your ma could teach me—"

Above them, a scraping noise shattered their reverie. It sounded as if something heavy was being dragged across the floor.

They glanced toward the narrow, winding staircase that rose from the narthex to the choir loft. William had never been up to the choir loft. Ma had, once, to clean up there in preparation for Easter, but he'd never been allowed to ascend the stairs.

"Too dangerous," Ma had said once when he'd asked. He'd been so young then though. Surely Stanislaw and Zofia hadn't been to the loft either. They'd only ever been to their Polish church.

Scree . . . eet.

William tensed, the hairs on the back of his neck standing on end, and not from the cold.

"What was that?" Zofia asked, her eyes wide but their bright blue subdued in the relative darkness.

"Who's up there?" Stanislaw gave William a

questioning look. "There's no Holy Mass tonight, is there?"

William shook his head. The church was open for visits all hours of the day and night, but no one would be in the loft. Only the pipe organ was up there, as far as he knew.

"Let's go see," Stanislaw said, rising and tugging Zofia to her feet. "Something made that sound."

Obviously. But William was content not knowing. Surely, the storm would pass soon. The rain would slow any minute, and they could make a run for it.

"I don't think we should—" William started, but already Stanislaw had climbed three steps, tugging Zofia behind him by the sleeve.

William glanced about at the gray stone and marble, the dark doors to the nave, and the dull stained glass window opposite him depicting a stern St. Michael, sword in hand.

Not wanting to be left behind, William scurried up the steps behind Zofia, slowing as the staircase curved just beneath the entry to the loft. It was nearly dark except for reddish light coming from the nave and spilling through the open doorway from the main part of the loft, where the organ sat.

The small anteroom they entered lay bare, only a stack of hymnals on the floor and a small oak table with a pair of ladies' gloves on it. A creak and a sound like the flutter of beating wings came from their left, and they turned, Zofia backing into William.

William clasped her arm, his heart pounding ridiculously fast. He recalled Dennis's jest about the púca, his chest tightening and his breaths quickening.

"Let's go," Zofia whispered. "We shouldn't be up here."

Another creak, and what William had thought to be paneling on the wall moved. The paneling, apparently, was a door—and it was opening!

A stale musty smell with an acrid overtone permeated the room, and William raised a hand to his nose.

Wings beat loudly as a bird emerged from the doorway, a soft yellow glow backlighting it as it flapped erratically around the room.

Zofia gasped, stumbling backward into William as a dark creature darted across the floor, toward the organ. Its long, fluffy tail flicked as it rounded the corner.

"The púca," William breathed, before turning and racing down the steps, nearly tripping as he made the final turn into the narthex. He hadn't waited for his friends but could feel Zofia's hand on his back at intervals and assumed Stanislaw was behind her.

But as the heavy exterior church doors closed behind him and Zofia, he realized his other friend hadn't followed. "Where's Stanislaw?" he asked Zofia, his heart still racing.

"I don't know. I-I followed you." The holy cards had been squeezed in her fist, and now she spread them across her palm, trying to flatten them.

What had happened to Stanislaw? Had the púca tricked him? William had seen the black cat. That flick of the tail had given it away. Had it been the shape-shifting púca?

The door behind them opened, and Stanislaw slid out,

looking a little pale but not as terrified as William probably appeared.

"Where were you?" William asked.

"I wanted to see where the sound came from," he said. "It was just a pigeon flapping. Probably got in at the belfry and made its way down. It looked like a narrow hallway behind the door. I don't know. There were a couple stairs going up . . ." He bit his lip. "I was going to go up, but, uh," he stalled, not able to meet William's gaze, "I thought I should come down and make sure you were okay. So, are you? Uh, okay?" Stanislaw shifted from foot to foot, fingers curling and uncurling in an uncharacteristically fidgety manner.

"We're fine," Zofia said, "but let's get out of here." She thrust the holy cards back into her pocket and started down the steps toward the street.

The storm had cleared and the sky brightened, if only a little. A sense of normalcy returned as they walked, deciding to abandon their plans for going door to door in William's neighborhood. The weather and the late hour had ruined that.

William silently chided himself for acting like a frightened child. It had only been a bird and a cat. Like Stanislaw said, the pigeon probably came in through the bell tower. And the cat, well, surely there were mice in the church. And birds, obviously. And bats. It would be a good hunting ground for a hungry alley cat.

But that yellow glow behind the door . . . Where had that come from?

The next morning, in the light of day, William cringed recalling how he'd fled the church. The cat they'd seen wasn't the púca. The púca wasn't even real. It had been a plain old, ordinary cat. The cat had probably been more frightened than them, especially with that dirty pigeon flapping all over the place. He hoped it had returned to the belfry and wouldn't be flapping around the church during morning Mass.

He'd lain awake last night, replaying the whole thing, admonishing himself but also wondering. Wondering what had created the yellow glow. There hadn't been enough moonlight to create that kind of light, even if it could've seeped in somehow from the roof or belfry. Surely, there were no candles or lanterns up there where they could set the whole building on fire! What could it have been? He hadn't imagined it, he was sure.

There was only one way to find out.

"Ma, can I run over to St. Columba for a visit?" What Irish Catholic mother would refuse her son a pious visit to the Blessed Sacrament? Not his.

"With your chores not done?" she asked as she sat cradling his half-asleep youngest brother, whose lanky legs hung limply over her lap. "We'll be going to Holy Mass later this morning, for the Feast of All Saints."

She wouldn't refuse him, would she? "I know. Please, Ma?"

She glanced around the kitchen, probably cataloging all the chores needing done. He and Dennis were often tasked with splitting wood for the fire. "All right. But be quick about it. And pray for your dear da's soul. And your sister's."

"Always," he said, springing from his seat and trying to ignore the pain in his chest at the mention of Da. "Thank you, Ma. I'll get to work as soon as I get back."

Sunlight broke through the clouds, warming William's back as he jogged toward the church. It would be much warmer today. Unseasonably warm, he guessed.

Inside the church, he peered around the narthex and in the nave, making certain no one was about. No pious old lady making the Stations of the Cross. No vagrant sleeping in a pew. No priests or sacristans fussing around the altar.

Quiet enough for a quick visit before his investigation. He genuflected, slid into the back pew, and dropped onto the hard kneeler. Bowing his head, he dutifully recited three Hail Marys for his sister's and his da's souls.

So little of Da remained for William to cling to. Most of his things had been sold or given away, and they'd lost touch with his family in Ireland years ago. There'd been the prospect of an uncle coming to America, but they'd heard nothing of that since they'd left Philadelphia, before Da's death.

Afraid that his solitude in the church would be short-lived, William blessed himself and exited to the narthex.

Confident the coast was clear, he climbed the winding staircase, his hand gliding over the cool wooden rail, his steps slowing as he neared the top. In the light of day, the anteroom appeared less ominous. The dusty hymnals sat where they had the night before. The ladies' gloves—a dingy white pair—lay on the table.

He peered at the paneling, open just a crack, no visible light emanating from the aperture.

With careful, quiet steps, William padded toward the paneling door. The musty odor he'd smelled last night made him wrinkle his nose. Pigeon droppings and mildew, most likely. A revolting combination.

With a finger, he gently pried the door open wide enough to see inside. No light came from the narrow walkway, which, as Stanislaw had said, rose by several steps into a narrow catwalk (literally, he supposed, as he'd seen the cat). The brick on the left must've been the inside of the exterior wall, making the dirty and unpainted plaster on the right the opposite side of the church's interior wall. Based on the height of the choir loft, he must've been somewhere above the tall stained glass windows, where the walls curved inward to meet the ceiling. The wooden plank floor didn't quite meet the walls but posed no threat of falling to anything larger than vermin.

Something rattled ahead of him, stopping William in his tracks, and a little of last night's fear returned, causing his heart rate to tick up. He breathed deeply to calm his nerves, then stifled a gagging cough when the wretched odors penetrated his lungs.

Something slammed, as if a heavy object had fallen far inside, along the catwalk, and William staggered back, fearful not so much of supernatural things but of an angry pastor or evil interloper who might not appreciate

William's presence.

He stepped backward slowly . . . carefully . . . then returned the paneled door to its former position. As he did so, something on the floor caught his eye. A small rectangle of paper.

He stooped and picked it up, turning it over in his hands. A holy card decorated with a chalice, candlesticks, and Easter lilies. A prayer, he presumed, was printed in the center in an alphabet he did not recognize. Zofia must have dropped it last night in their haste to leave. He recalled her clutching her cards in her hands.

A whoosh of air, as if from a bellows, came from the main loft, and William turned and dashed down the stairs and out the doors into the street, where he stood for a moment, catching his breath.

He must've been imagining the yellow glow after all. Nothing besides some pigeons and a cat would venture onto that walkway. What was it meant for, anyway, a hidden walkway so high above the altar it nearly touched the roof? Whatever the case, the sounds he'd heard today could've been anything. Maybe the bricks up there had been loosened with all of that animal activity. The cat might have knocked something over. Maybe someone had been in the main loft too, at the organ.

William spun the holy card in his hand and studied the pictures and the strange words. He'd return it to Zofia. Maybe next year they'd just stay home and hand out soul cakes with the holy cards on All Hallows' Eve.

William tried to concentrate during Holy Mass. Truly, he did. But through the first part of the liturgy, his mind and his gaze were drawn to the rafters. To what might lie behind the walls. Because try as he might to dismiss his curiosity, he wondered.

In his homily, Father McCann spoke of all the great intercessors in heaven. The men and women, boys and girls, who'd lived their lives with great faith and courage—some to the point of martyrdom. William's heart swelled with an eagerness to emulate their holiness, a holiness that even the greatest sinners could achieve through the merits of God's grace.

He thought, too, of Zofia's holy cards and wondered about the stories of the Polish saints. He'd have to learn more about them.

As his family spilled out of the church following Mass, intent on getting home to celebrate the feast day the best way they knew how—with a big meal!—William asked if he could first return the holy card he'd found to Zofia.

"Don't you be dawdlin'," Ma ordered. "If you're not at the table, one of your brothers or sisters may eat your share."

It wasn't an idle threat. It had happened before. "Yes, Ma. I'll be quick!"

William ran the several blocks to his friends' house, a balmy breeze lifting his hair. Outside their house, the sweet smell of yeast bread made William's stomach rumble. He'd make it a quick visit for sure and get home for breakfast!

Stanislaw opened the door, Zofia at his heels.

"I was back at the church today, of course, for the holy day." His friends had attended Holy Mass this morning too, based on the Sunday best they wore. He left out the story of his early morning visit and got right to the point. "I found one of your holy cards," he said, extending it to Zofia. "You must've dropped it last night as we were, uh, leaving."

Zofia's brow wrinkled, but she accepted the card and examined it. "This isn't mine," she said, handing it back to William. "I don't have one with a chalice on it."

"You don't?" William took it back, puzzled. If the card didn't belong to Zofia, where had it come from? Had it been lying there for God knew how long? Or had someone else dropped it more recently? Maybe someone who'd been in the catwalk. With the yellow light.

"Zofia!" his friends' mother called from inside the house.

"I've got to go," she said. "It's a pretty card, but it's not mine." Then she turned and walked back into the house.

"Stanislaw," William said, his curiosity piqued even as the hairs on his neck pricked. "Can you meet me at St. Columba tomorrow morning? I want to find out what's behind that door." Or who.

"Yeah, uh, if you want to." Stanislaw seemed reluctant but probably didn't want William to see his fear.

They said their farewells, and William hustled home, so intent on getting to breakfast he almost didn't notice the black cat that crossed his path. Almost.

William awoke early on All Souls' Day, up before the sun. And his family. He hadn't slept well anyway, worrying about waking on time. Dennis had been talking about the púca again, scaring Margaret and their other little siblings with his made-up stories of a man-eater disguised as a dark horse until Ma had told him in no uncertain terms to shut his trap!

Whether Ma believed the stories about the púca, he wasn't sure. She and Da had told them about the púca, after all, but they'd done it with winks and smiles across the kitchen table. They had faith in God, not in superstition and folklore. Yes, there were supernatural realities, the Church made that plain. But God was in His heaven, and His children should not fear. That was all through the Gospels: "Be not afraid."

Da would probably chide him for being afraid. He and his brother had been afraid of nothing—including the púca, according to his tales.

William dressed quickly and quietly, then padded down the steps and out the front door, closing it with a soft click. He wasn't sneaking, exactly. He'd told Ma he was meeting Stanislaw early. The whole house didn't need to know.

A few minutes later, he spotted Stanislaw standing at the foot of the steps of St. Columba. He shuffled from foot to foot, hands in and out of his pockets as his gaze darted about.

William greeted his anxious friend with a wave and a "good morning" and they headed inside the cool, dark church.

Up the winding staircase they went, Stanislaw trailing William this time. Again, William's heart began pounding, the silence buzzing in his ears.

What would they find this morning? A pigeon? A cat? Something . . . else?

The loft on their right appeared dark and empty. The hymnals and gloves, still in the same places. The door camouflaged by the paneling was open only a crack, as evidenced by the yellow glow emanating from it.

William stopped in his tracks, a shiver running down his spine. The heat of Stanislaw's body pressed in on him from behind, and despite the cool temperature, a sweat broke out on William's forehead.

The púca is not real. I'm not a child. I don't believe in superstitions. I trust in God alone.

With a fortifying breath—a shallow one because of the odor—William stepped forward until his fingers touched the door. He uttered a silent prayer for protection to every saint he could call to mind—even those Polish ones—then pried open the door.

He climbed the steep steps, that yellow glow illuminating his path.

One . . .

Two . . .

Three . . . and the catwalk stretched out in front of him.

Several yards in, drawings of some sort on the wall caught his attention. He stretched the collar of his shirt over his nose and mouth and brushed a hand over the images.

Holy cards. Tacked to the wall with nails, small and large, hammered in haphazardly but creating a shrine of sorts to various saints and honoring the Holy Family and the Blessed Sacrament.

"What is this place?" Stanislaw whispered, his warm breath tickling William's ear.

William shrugged. He had no idea.

"Hey, look!" Stanislaw tugged his sleeve, turning him to the opposite wall. A few photographs hung there, one battered, alongside a few pencil sketches of men and women, none of whom William recognized. Random, ordinary people, it looked like.

Except . . . one photo caught his eye. Two young men, shirtsleeves rolled up, posing with sickles in hand in front of a field of grain. So familiar.

William leaned in. Was that a young version of his da?

"Who's there?" a rough and ragged voice called from deep within the catwalk.

The yellow light dimmed and wobbled, creating a kaleidoscope of flickering light on the walls, ceiling, and floor.

"Let's go!" Stanislaw urged, tugging at William's sleeve.

But William's gazed fixed to the photo. He shrugged off his friend's hand. "You go," he said, his eyes still trained on the two men with sickles.

One hand released him and another, stronger hand grabbed William, turning him toward the flickering light.

A lantern hung from the hand of a skinny, scruffy man,

his face half hidden in shadows. "What are you doing?"

William's breath hitched. This was no fairytale monster. No shape shifter. This was a man. Not a particularly tough-looking man, but man enough to overpower William. Why had William come here? A missing prayer card, a sliver of yellow light—was his curiosity surrounding these insignificant things worth what may happen to him at the hands of this . . . hobo?

The man stared, his eyes narrowing as he lifted the lantern higher, illuminating William's face.

William turned away, the light blinding him.

A rough hand guided his chin back until he was staring at a pair of familiar-looking blue eyes. He couldn't grasp the memory, but the eyes . . .

"Are you kin to Jeremiah Cook?" the hobo said with a thick Irish accent.

Jeremiah Cook? That was—

"That's . . . that's me da's name." William's breaths came short and quick. "I'm William. I'm his son."

The man moved the lantern from side to side, examining William's face from all angles. "I see it. Yes, yes." He laughed, a genuine, joyous laugh. "I *thought* he'd gone west. I just hadn't found my way to you yet."

William's brow wrinkled. Found his way? What did he mean by that?

"William, I'm . . ." A smile spread across his face. "I'm your uncle."

Once the shock wore off, for both William and Uncle

James, there was some explaining to do to Father McCann. Apparently, Stanislaw had caused some commotion in his flight down the steps, nearly colliding with the priest at the bottom.

Then it had been William's turn to explain, and, finally, Uncle James, who'd spent the last five nights sleeping in the belfry loft of the Irish church with Father McCann's tacit approval. Uncle James had arrived in New York City alone only weeks before, traveling south and then west in hopes of finding harbor with his deceased brother's family.

Father McCann sent William home to retrieve his ma, who'd come in a hurry to identify Uncle James, who she'd last seen when she and Da had left Ireland nearly two decades before.

Once everything had been set-to-rights, Uncle James came home to the Cook family, to all his brother's living children. He'd spent the last lonely days in a strange country, with only the saints in heaven and the souls of his beloved family and friends as his other-worldly companions, but now, he embraced his flesh-and-blood family with smiles, tears, and oh-so-many tales of Ireland and his voyage.

As the Cooks made their way to the cemetery to visit Da's grave, William followed close behind Ma and Uncle James, Dennis at his side. Leaves stirred and fell from the trees as a gentle breeze blew.

The sight of Uncle James, the timbre of his voice, even his gait, gave form to William's fuzzy memories of Da, and he thanked God for his uncle's arrival.

They shuffled through the leaf-covered grass beneath an old sycamore tree toward Da's headstone. Ma cleared the tangled, dying grass and pressed a kiss to the stone with her palm.

Uncle James choked up, sinking to his knees on Da's grave, weeping. Ma swiped tears from her eyes, and William and his brothers and sisters stayed quiet. Visiting Da's grave was always mournful, but this All Souls' Day, William's tears dried quickly, his heart filling with hope.

His silly fears had been unfounded. And his Uncle James, the hobo in the belfry, had reminded him of how thin the veil was between God's children here and beyond.

He recalled Zofia's holy cards and the cards Uncle James had tacked along the catwalk—holy heavenly intercessors. Great saints, the Holy Family, and Jesus Himself in the sacraments. And then his extended family. His da, his sister Anne (though she was likely in heaven already), and all the family members who had gone before them—even those he'd never known.

William pressed his eyes shut and prayed, grateful for God's goodness in providing him with such a family—his own and that of the Church.

Face tilted to the weak November sunlight, William opened his eyes just in time to see a black tail swish and slip behind a headstone.

###

Irish immigrants to America brought variations of Hallowtide customs with them, including souling, in which poor children (sometimes in costume) would go door-to-door seeking a treat, like a soul cake, in exchange for prayers for the deceased or a little entertainment, such as singing.

Irish immigrants also brought their Celtic folklore, including stories of the púca, a mischievous shapeshifting creature alternately depicted as either menacing or benevolent. The púca commonly appeared as a dark animal such as a horse, cat, rabbit, or dog.

ABOUT THE AUTHOR

CAROLYN ASTFALK writes from the sweetest place on earth, Hershey, Pennsylvania, where she lives with her husband and four children. In addition to her contemporary Catholic romances, including the young adult coming-of-age story *Rightfully Ours*, she is a CatholicMom.com contributor. She is a past president of the Catholic Writers Guild. When she is not washing dishes, doing laundry, or reading, you can find her blogging about books, faith, and family life at www.CarolynAstfalk.com.

3

A VERY JURASSIC HALLOWTIDE

by Corinna Turner

HARRY

"The drifts are even higher this morning," I say to Josh, trying to sound casual as I peer through the window of the Habitat Vehicle's living area. It's still dark, but Josh has the shutters open despite the cold, probably because the full moon is making everything look downright ethereal. Or maybe he's keeping an eye out for that boisterous pack of juvenile T. rex that got us into this mess by halfway ripping off one of the vehicle's continuous snow tracks—apparently for the sheer fun of it.

Josh shrugs and goes back to eating oatmeal. If it worries him that we've been trapped here in this unseasonably early blizzard for over a week now, he doesn't show it. But there's no ignoring the fact that an immobilized HabVi is a vulnerable HabVi. Our armor won't keep out a rex.

I'm just sitting down with a bowl of my own when my

big sister, Darryl, emerges from her little over-cab bedroom. She's fully dressed, rifle in hand, ready for the day, her long brown hair in its usual braid—and, just like us, she's wearing her parka indoors to save fuel. She leans the gun against the wall beside mine and shoots me a glance. I am up far earlier than normal, but I jerked awake wondering if the Habitat Vehicle had been completely buried in cold whiteness yet.

Technicolor—the HabVi owned by Josh's best friends and almost-uncles, West, Thiago, and Ed—was hoping to get up here with a new track for us by tonight—All Hallows' Eve. But the relentless blizzard combined with damp soft snow because of the—comparatively—warm temperatures has made the trip into the mountains too dangerous. My heart sinks yet again—we were all looking forward to spending the Hunter Festival of the Dead with Technicolor. Hunters take Hallowtide even more seriously than farmers like me and Darryl—and way more seriously than city-Catholics.

Although, one year, Father Ben did take us in-city for a "souling" trip where we were in full competition with the trick-or-treaters as we went door-to-door, offering to pray for the dead. We were allowed to accept thank-you candy, so it was great!

"Are you sure Technicolor can't get to us?" I ask.

Josh shakes his head, making his shaggy black hair swing slightly. "I told them not to even try. Not this far into the mountains. Ain't worth it. This early snow will melt any day now. Or it will get colder, and the going will be good."

"And if it doesn't?" I can't help demanding.

"Then, sure, they'll come up to us. But it will be slow and chancy." He looks out the window and smiles. "In fact, let's bag a few of those leggy'saurs; save our remaining supplies."

JOSHUA

The leggy'saurs ain't wary of the 'Vi. By the time I'm satisfied the surrounding area is clear of danger, and we'll be able to retrieve our kills, the sun is almost up and the leggy'saurs are rooting under the snow for grass at the far end of our little valley, still nicely in sight. We all drop one, and Darryl and I drop two more as they bolt, though Harry misses his second shot.

"They ain't called leggy'saurs for nothing," I say, to make him feel better. "Real fast when they get moving."

"Sure are," mutters Harry, his green eyes glum. But as I open my mouth again, he leaps up and puts his foot on the ladder down from the observation turret. "*I'll* go bring them in." He looks eagerly to me for permission, keen as ever to prove himself.

I try not to smile. If he wants to heave five dog-sized leggy'saurs all the way to the 'Vi, I ain't stopping him.

"I'll help," says Darryl, amusement in her blue eyes, but I shake my head.

"No. Those juvenile rex are still around. We need two of us to provide cover. Harry, pass the rex gun up 'fore you go out, 'kay?"

Harry swallows, like he's a bit less keen to get out there all of a sudden. But he nods and heads below. While he opens the gun cabinet and passes the hefty gun up to Darryl, I re-launch the drone and check on the fractious pack of juveniles. But they're still a good distance away. I re-inspect the rest of the area: quiet. Even larger herbi'saurs will keep clear of rex.

"Okay, Harry, clear."

HARRY

I lower myself down carefully from the side-door, then trudge off along the little valley. The snow is soon up to my knees. No wonder Josh was amused that I was so keen to come out. Never mind. If I can carry two leggy'saurs at once, I only need to do three trips.

But when I finally reach the carcasses and start lifting the first one, Darryl's voice immediately comes over my earpiece. "If you put that thing over your shoulder, I'm going to disown you, Harry."

My cheeks get really hot. "Oh, come on. It's no distance at all, and you two are both right there. Who cares if I get a smear of blood on me? If I can't put one on my shoulder, I'll have to make five trips."

"So, make five trips." Josh's tone leaves no room for argument.

Sighing loudly to make my opinion clear, I grab two leggy'saurs' featherless tails instead and start towing them through the snow. Heck, these skinny things are heavier than they look. All that muscle.

I trudge on, dragging just one. Why did I volunteer? I bet Josh would have gone. He's nineteen and so much bigger and stronger. Even Darryl, at seventeen, is still larger than I am.

I heave the carcass into the 'Vi and head back out again.

Repeat.

Repeat.

Repeat.

Just one to go, then I can get warm. The outcrop that's sheltering the 'Vi from the worst of the weather extends along this side of the valley, too, breaking the wind a little, but the cold is still creeping down the neck and up the sleeves of my parka. I'm almost to the final leggy'saur when Josh speaks, quick and clear. *"Orange."*

My heart jolts in shock. *Codeword!* Josh has drilled us over and over: *Pick up any gear and run back to the 'Vi.*

I hesitate. Does the carcass count as gear?

"Leave it." Josh's voice is sharper this time. Then suddenly, he snaps, *"Red!"*

Red: drop everything, leave anything, sprint!

I haven't anything to drop, but I lurch forward through the thick snow, trying to achieve something like an actual run.

"Those rex are heading this way, so hurry up." Josh gives me more information now that I'm in motion. "They hadn't been going too fast, but then they went up a gear."

The five or six juveniles are already huge. My heart pounds twice as hard as I stumble on. Hah, I'm back to the clearer bit of slope. I try to speed up, but in the next moment, I'm tumbling. A snowbank breaks my fall. I lie dazed for a second.

"Harry? You okay?" Darryl's voice.

"Harry, get up." Josh, sounding stern. "*Move.*"

I roll onto my knees and start to rise. Pain stabs through my ankle, and I collapse back into the snow, reaching for it with my gloved hands. "*Agh. Ow.* My ankle!" Is it broken?

"How bad?" demands Josh.

"I can't stand on it! You have to come help me!"

"No time for that. Crawl a few feet to your left, worm your way under that overhang, and lie still, 'kay? No blood on you, right?"

I let go of my ankle to cast a frantic glance over my gloves and forearms. "No! But—"

"Drop your gloves, just in case. You'll be fine." Josh sounds very calm and firm again. "The rex won't notice you. Just get in there and don't move."

I gulp, looking around for the hidey-hole as the 'Vi's too-far-distant side door hisses closed and locks. There. Some rock has crumbled away at the bottom of the outcrop near me, leaving an overhanging part. Abandoning my nice warm gloves, I crawl through the snow on hands and knees, choking back any sound of pain as each movement jars my ankle.

In moments, I'm sliding into that dark slit on my stomach. I only just fit. The dirt under my cheek feels hard but dry compared to the snow—and is vibrating slightly. I lie still, panting with pain and exertion and . . . yeah, with fear too. I guess this situation wouldn't bother Josh, but I don't like it one bit.

Uh-oh . . . The first rex appears in my line of vision. Oh yeah, it's really running flat out. They all stream past, yep, six of them. The ground shakes under me, and they're not even full-grown. All male, of course. Females stay with their mothers until full adulthood.

I go on lying still. My heart's pounding so hard it's hurting me. My cold, wet hands dig into the dirt, making fists. A stick pokes one palm. I let the dirt filter soundlessly from my fingers and tighten my grip on the little twig.

Reaching the outcrop end of the valley, the pack swings in a big circle, tails brushing against the 'Vi. They pause for a moment, sniffing—can they smell the blood inside?—but then they're eagerly rushing back the other way, soon passing out of my field of vision. They're not even chasing anything, are they? Except each other.

The twig is so smooth. I stroke the smoothness with my thumb, trying to focus on it.

Ground shaking . . . the rex are back. One of them has the last leggy'saur in its mouth. Another one snatches at it, grabbing the hind quarters. The carcass tears in half, guts spilling everywhere. A third, smaller juvenile darts in to eat them, while the first two each swallow down their halves in a single gulp.

My own guts knot up and start to shake. That could've been me. Would they get their heads under here?

Just lie still, Harry. Lie still . . .

It's smooth. A beautiful smooth little twig. How long has it been lying here? I stroke it, turning it in my concealed hand. *Stroke, stroke, smooth, smooth . . .*

"Harry?" Josh's voice through my earpiece, sounding totally relaxed, snaps me out of my self-induced twig-trance. "All clear. I'll come and give you a hand back to the 'Vi."

DARRYL

And . . . Josh and Harry are in. Side door closed and locked. I slide quickly down the ladder.

"Harry, you okay? How's your ankle?"

"I—" His light skin is paler than usual. "I lost the last leggy'saur. I'm sorry."

"Hey, we weren't expecting you to fight no rex for it," says Josh lightly, rubbing his own darker skinned nose to restore circulation. "I told you to drop it, remember?"

"Come on, sit down," I tell Harry. "Let's take a look."

"It actually may just be sprained," Harry says, sinking down in a chair with a wince.

"Well, you couldn't have run on it, neither way," says Josh.

I check Harry's ankle as well as I can—nope, doesn't seem to be broken—then wrap it up well and make him put on an ankle-brace to keep the weight off it. You've got to climb up and down a lot, living in a HabVi.

"What's that?" I ask, since Harry's been clutching something ever since he climbed in.

"This? Oh, I thought it was a twig, but now I think it's a bone." He holds out his hand, showing us a smooth, creamy object. "Some kinda leg bone from a small 'saur, maybe? What kind, Josh?"

Slowly, Josh reaches out and takes the bone from him.

One look at his face . . .

It's no dinosaur bone.

JOSHUA

"What do you mean it's *human*?" Harry stares at me in horror. "You're kidding, right? Hunters play All Hallows' Eve pranks, do they?"

"It's human," I repeat. I reach out and touch his second finger. "This one. From an adult. Probably a man, from the length."

"You're *serious*?" Harry jumps up, hobbles to the sink, and starts washing his hands vigorously.

"How did it get out here?" asks Darryl, clearly more prepared to take my word for it.

I examine it for a moment, judging the age, my gut twisting painfully. "I think I know. There were some hunters my dad and uncle knew when I were very little. Technicolor knew 'em much better. I barely remember 'em, but there were the one guy, Lenny Miller, who owned the HabVi, and there were the other guy, Tidna Way, his long-term assistant and friend. Well, he thought Tidna were his friend. Lenny had no family, so he made Tidna his heir in his will. Bad move. Shortly after Lenny finally saved up enough for a nice new HabVi, Tidna killed him. Right here in this valley."

Harry stares at me, open-mouthed. "I don't know which is more awful, that Tidna *did* that, or that *you* parked us here!"

I stare at him, confused. "It's the best shelter for miles. Why shouldn't we park here?"

Harry shakes his head and mutters, *"hunters"* in that way of his that makes it sound like some sorta swearword.

"But . . ." Darryl stares at the bone in my hand. "Didn't they recover the body?"

I shake my head. "Nope. So this likely belongs to poor Lenny." I head to the gun cabinet, fish out an empty little ammo box, line it with a scrap of nice hide, and place the bone carefully inside. "I guess we should either bury it or give it to Father Ben next time we see him."

"Shouldn't we, like, hand it in to the authorities or something?" says Harry.

"No point."

"Might help them catch Tidna."

"Doubt that."

"Why?"

"Because Tidna's dead too."

HARRY

In a way, I'm lucky I twisted my ankle, because I get to sit down while Josh and Darryl skin and butcher all the carcasses. Soon the meat is in the too-empty freeze-dryer, with a little in the fridge for immediate consumption, and the unusable parts have gone into the incinerator. They hose everything down and clean thoroughly. And then they clean some more. Hunters are obsessed with cleaning, anyway, to prevent the build-up of tasty smells that might draw predators, and they always clean extra before big feasts.

But I get to sit in a chair and watch for once. I try not to glance at the gun cabinet too often. Josh put the bone in there. I wipe my hand on my pants yet again. I can't believe I was *stroking* that thing. *Ugh.*

After a good lunch of leggy'saur stew, they set to work decorating for tonight. Soon, bones, claws, teeth, and feathers adorn every door and ledge and anywhere something can be fastened or persuaded to stay. Above all, bones. Lots of bones.

"I'm surprised you don't stick Lenny's bone up somewhere too," I mutter as Josh arranges yet another femur right over the door into his cab bedroom.

Josh frowns at me. "That would be very disrespectful."

"Human bodies should be treated with reverence," says Darryl, staring at me. "Surely, you remember Father Ben telling us that?"

My ankle aches fiercely, and I'm having trouble getting back into the mood for tonight. I spread my hands. "*Joke!*"

"Harry, do you want to go take a nap?" asks Darryl. "You seem kinda out of sorts."

"Out of sorts? Oh, really? I almost got eaten this morning!"

Josh snorts. "Almost got et? *Hardly.* Their heads wouldn't fit into that gap. You were almost as safe as you'd be in the 'Vi."

I chuck a velociraptor pelvis at him—*almost as . . . ?* But he simply catches it—"Oh yeah. Just what I need to finish this off"—and goes back to his decorating.

Hunters.

DARRYL

By the time darkness falls, everything is ready. Pictures of our dead loved ones—all decorated with beautiful raptor ruff feathers—have been placed all around: either physical photos or images on the console screen or the paused photo frame. Josh's dad and his uncle Z, Mom and our grandparents, and others from both families. Unlit candles stand ready in front of them, while Josh and I have just finished lighting the candles placed all around.

The rest of the 'Vi is an impressive thicket of bones and feathers and claws and teeth. I can imagine how good it would look with evergreens too, but we couldn't get any with those rex prowling. We've baked a precise quantity of tiny, rich soul cakes for the hunter souling ceremony, and Josh has dug out a small physical prayer book of his dad's that contains the liturgy for the dead.

"Okay, guess we're ready," says Josh, grinning as he switches off the electric lights, plunging us into flickering candlelight.

Harry looks up with more excitement than he's shown for hours. We won't eat anything tonight except the soul cakes—that's how hunters do All Hallows' Eve, apparently. But Josh, bless him, plonked a large sandwich down in front of Harry shortly before the sun set and told him to eat up because he was injured—and now Harry's much more cheerful.

My stomach's growling, but we do the liturgy first, taking it in turns to read from the book as we pray for the dead generally, and our dead in particular. Josh doesn't hurry, leaving lots of gaps for us to pray silently. We're supposed to keep this vigil until midnight, and dusk to midnight is a long period at this time of year.

"Don't you think Mom's already in heaven?" Harry asks, when we've finished the book-prayers and take a break to drink some boiling water with honey—another hunter tradition. "She was so . . . so nice. *And* holy. Wasn't she?" Harry was very young when Mom died. I'm not surprised he sounds questioning, like he doesn't quite trust his memories.

"Yeah, and I really hope she is," I say. "But remember what Father Ben said? That if you think about the infinite goodness of God, then *comparatively* speaking, even a tiny little sin isn't that much different than murder from God's perspective."

"So . . . how long do we keep praying for her?" Harry asks.

Josh's brown eyes widen. "Hunters never stop praying for their dead. Why would you even wanna? Nothing impure can be in God's presence, right? So everything that ain't perfect's gonna have to go before they can actually be with Him. And if it's like *burning* . . ." Grim-faced, he shakes his head. "Nope, I ain't stopping. There's no *time* there. It's always gonna do good."

"Father Ben says the purification may be more like longing," I say. "Like, a longing for union with God that's so intense it's kinda equivalent to pain. But not actually pain."

Josh brightens. "Thiago thinks purgatory's like getting to the doorway of heaven and God's *right there*, just inside, so close, but no bad can go in, so it all burns away in a flash. So, it ain't *how long* it takes—no time there anyways—it's just *how much* there is to burn off. But mebbe it's how much you *wanna* go in that, like, burns it away."

"But whatever *we* pray away *for* them doesn't have to be, like, burned or longing-ed away?" Harry checks.

"Yep," Josh says and drinks the last of his honeyed water in one gulp. "So, let's get back to it."

HARRY

The souling is much less formal than the liturgy. Josh starts, so we can see what to do, gathering us around the photo of his dad and uncle. He lights three candles and takes two soul cakes from the tray. Bigger than a walnut but smaller than an apricot, they're glazed in a smooth, pale sugar wash that reflects the candlelight in a suitably ghostly manner.

Josh offers one to Darryl. "Of your mercy, please pray for the soul of Isaiah Wilson, and take this cake to sustain you."

She accepts it, and he says the same to me, handing me the other one. We eat the cakes—umm, they're just as nice as the couple of spoons I got to lick earlier—then kneel silently around the photo frame for some time. Well, they kneel; I sit in my chair because of my ankle. Then Josh asks us to pray for his Uncle Z—Zechariah Wilson—and hands us two more cakes.

And so it goes on. In the flickering candlelight, surrounded by the beauty of the feathers and the mortality of the bones, claws, and teeth, we slowly, quietly, make our way around our dead.

And . . . we're finished. Right? Still twenty minutes until midnight—Josh has mistimed it. Or is there some kind of closing prayer ritual?

But no. I can't see a picture, but Josh is lighting more candles. Uh-oh, it's *the* bone. I hadn't even noticed it there.

Josh picks up the final two soul cakes. "Of your mercy, please pray for Lenny Miller—or the soul of this bone— and take this cake to sustain you."

I break the tiny cake—dark under its sugar coating— and eat it slowly in two bites to savor it better, since it's the last one. Then, for another twenty minutes, we pray for the soul that goes with this bone. Okay, mostly my mind wanders, and I almost nod off three times. But whenever I remember what we're doing, I say another prayer.

It's midnight. Finally. The candles are still burning, and I'm not convinced Josh is going to go straight to bed. And if he doesn't, Darryl might not either. But I can barely keep my eyes open, and my ankle still hurts a lot. Without showering or even brushing my teeth, I ease my boots off, then climb awkwardly up to my cupboard bunk—thank God for the brace!

I just manage to maneuver my aching ankle carefully

into my sleeping bag before putting my head on my pillow . . .

When I open my eyes, flickering candlelight reflects on the wall of my bunk. I forgot to close the little sliding door. I must've been tired. From the silence, it's still the middle of the night. I'll close it and go back to sleep.

But when I roll over to shut the door, a figure is looking in at me through the little opening, so close I could touch him. A guy, maybe mid-twenties, wearing typical hunter clothing. Only a shirt, no parka. Isn't he cold? He's simply there, staring silently at me.

His face . . . claw marks score one cheek. Blood stains his shirt too. One hand looks badly bitten. I've never seen him before in my life.

I should be terrified.

But I'm not.

JOSHUA

I jerk awake at the scuff and clang of Harry climbing awkwardly down from his bunk. *Oops.* I haven't quite toppled over onto the floor, the way Darryl did a while ago, but I were definitely dozing. I were gonna pray until all the candles burned out, the way my family always has.

Curled up in front of her family photos, Darryl stirs too, pushing aside the blanket I laid over her.

"Gonna pray some more, Harry?" I ask.

Harry ignores me. "Who *is* he?"

"Who?"

"The guy."

"What guy?" I glance around automatically. "There's no one here but us."

"But he was—" Harry breaks off, his face wrinkling up in confusion. "There's really no one here?"

"You must've been dreaming, Harry," says Darryl, yawning as she sits up and wraps the blanket around her, shivering slightly in the night's cold.

"No, I wasn't. I had just woken up when I saw him."

"It's possible to dream that you've woken up," points out Darryl.

"I was *awake*. There was a guy, a stranger, looking into my berth. He didn't speak; he was just staring at me. And ... it was really weird. I wasn't scared of him. Even though he was all cut up and bloodied and stuff."

"What?" I speak more sharply. "You weren't afraid of him, and he were all cut up? Like, by an animal?"

"Yeah."

"What did he look like?"

Darryl shoots me a puzzled look.

"He was ... er ... mostly white, I guess. Maybe a bit of something else. Dark hair? Normal hunter clothes. And his face, his chest, his hand—all mauled. Big claw marks. Large raptor?"

The hairs rise on end all down my back. I get up off my knees and move to the console, swiping to the photo archive. I'm worried how far back I'll have to go, but a simple search by name throws up results.

"Josh?" says Darryl, peering over my shoulder. "Harry

just had a dream, right?"

"Harry"—he's already hanging over my other shoulder—"look at this photo."

I open the file.

Harry peers closer at the group shot—then gasps. "That's him!"

DARRYL

"*What?*" Confusion—and disbelief—fills me as I glance at my little brother. "Has Harry seen that photo before?"

"Never," says Harry firmly—and a little defiantly. "Still think I was asleep?"

"Who ... who is that?" I ask, though part of me anticipates the answer.

"Lenny Miller," says Josh.

Yep. I glance at the bone. The three candles, the last lit, still flicker.

I turn back to Josh. "How did you know?"

Josh shrugs. "Well, it weren't no live man, that's for sure. And as soon as Harry said he hadn't been afraid, though he shoulda been ... Well, that's the number one sign of a soul in purgatory asking for prayers."

"Is it?"

Josh shrugs again. "It's the test hunters apply, anyways. If it ain't frightening, it's probably just a soul. If it is scary, or it tries to talk to you, then mebbe it's a demon trying to trick you."

"So ..." Growing belatedly pale and shaken, Harry stammers, "W-what do we do?"

Yet another shrug from Josh. "Pray for him, of course."

HARRY

"Pray, yeah." Silly me! "Guess that's exactly what we should do. So, should we say, like, a Rosary or something?"

"I think it calls for a bit more than a Rosary." Darryl laughs. "And we should definitely message Father Ben and ask him to say Mass too."

"Let's fast until the end of the Triduum," says Josh, without hesitation. "And take the two days for soul days. Keep a vigil too."

My heart sinks like a box of ammo chucked into a pond. "But what about the Solemnity of All Saints? I thought it was a major feast day. So, shouldn't we, well, *feast*?"

"A soul just appeared to you asking for prayers. I think that takes priority. Let's feast all the saints when Technicolor finally get up here."

I look pleadingly at Darryl. She twists her lip uncertainly. "It's strongly *advised* to feast on feast days, but I don't think it's actually forbidden to do it the other way around. I mean, will we even feel like celebrating until we've done something for this poor murdered guy?"

My turn to bite my lip. Would I enjoy all the tasty things we've been saving for All Saints, knowing that solemn-eyed guy is suffering something, somewhere? Perfectly just, purifying suffering, sure, but if God let him appear to me like that, I guess we're meant to help him.

My sigh comes out bigger than I intend. "Fine. It's a

plan."

"You don't have to, of course," says Josh. "You're only fourteen."

"Hey! Who did Lenny appear to, again?"

JOSHUA

"So, what actually happened to Lenny?" asks Darryl in the morning, after we've done some prayer in place of breakfast. "I mean, if Tidna murdered him, why was the apparition all clawed up by a raptor?"

"Well, you could say that the raptor were the murder weapon," I reply. "Tidna didn't shoot him, if that's what you were thinking. Lenny were stalking some game, and Tidna were on watch. And a Utahraptor got Lenny's scent and stalked *him*. And Tidna just sat there and never said a word."

Darryl's eyes widen with horror, and Harry screws up his face.

"But Tidna *did* get caught?" says Harry fiercely.

"Yeah. It were West, Thiago, and Ed that found him. Apparently, on his way in-city, though at the time they arrived, he were dead drunk. First he told 'em Lenny were dead, that there'd been a terrible accident. Then he said it were all his fault, that he'd killed him. Well, they didn't take that seriously because any time there's an accident that bad, the survivors tend to feel guilty as heck. But what were suspicious were that it'd clearly been eight days before Tidna had even started on his way in-city to report the death."

Darryl and Harry look blankly back at me. "So?"

"So, in a real old 'Vi, like Lenny's original one, the camera data were only stored for seven days, then it were overwritten by the new stuff. What Tidna clearly didn't know were that a newer HabVi stored closer to three months of data. Anyways, West downloaded the system, just like he should in that situation, and they escorted Tidna to the Elders for the inquiry."

"They were really suspicious then," said Darryl. "Since Tidna was their friend too, right?"

"Nah, someone dies out in the wilds like that, alone with someone, it's always checked up on. They thought he'd just been too upset to get himself moving. Even when he kept on saying it were his fault, over and over, they didn't take him seriously until the Elders played the data from the console. And that showed it all. Footage of the raptor stalking Lenny, earpiece audio proving Tidna were awake, hadn't just dozed off at the wrong moment. Open and shut case. It were horrible for West, Thiago, and Ed. West were real good friends with Lenny, and Thiago with Tidna."

Thiago . . . so famous for being a grumpy worrier. For the first time it hits me . . . was he always like that? Or . . . ? A close friend kills another friend . . . how does that affect you?

"But," Harry says, dragging me from my moment of realization, "what *happened* to Tidna?"

DARRYL

"He's dead now." Josh's voice goes very uncommunicative, no surprise.

"Yeah, but how did he die?" demands Harry.

"I think we should keep up the prayer watch throughout the day too, don't you?" Josh glances at me. "I guess it's my turn."

"Sure, good idea," I say.

Harry directs me a frustrated look, but surely he knows by now that there's no point pestering Josh about hunter secrets, of which the ways of hunter justice are the deepest—and possibly darkest—of them all?

Normally, it would be nice to have a soul day—a retreat day, I guess Father Ben would call it. No work, no expectations to do anything but spiritual reading, formal prayer, or chilling out with God. But not having eaten properly since lunchtime yesterday is distracting. Harry ate more recently but keeps eyeing the food cupboards longingly. Josh seems unconcerned, but then hunters frequently miss one or even two meals on busy days.

I glance at the bone, around which we've kept candles burning, and shiver slightly. What a horrible story. How could someone be greedy enough to do something like that? To their best friend!

The murderer was dead drunk when Technicolor found him, though. And blaming himself. Even when he'd sobered up. So maybe he regretted it almost at once.

Too late for Lenny—and for him.

HARRY

My empty stomach screams for food. The sun has set now, but we're not supposed to eat until the end of tomorrow. Or the following morning? How will Josh calculate the end of the Triduum? This is way too hard core for me.

Josh and Darryl seem happy enough. Taking their turns at the prayer watch, or up in the privacy of the turret being one with God or nature or whatever. I take my turn too, but it's so hard to keep my mind on praying. I keep thinking about food. I've got out the *Memoirs of Saint Desmond* now, but I keep reading the same sentence over and over. Is this really helping Lenny?

Offer it up. I can almost hear Darryl saying it. Or Dad. Or Father Ben. Yeah, it'll help. If I want it to.

I've just got to stop thinking about food . . .

Poor Lenny. Did he have time to realize what had happened when that Utahraptor suddenly pounced on him, or was it over too quickly? I guess I know in my head there are people as evil as Tidna, but a real one is always a shock. Well, Tidna's rotting in hell, and God wants us to help poor Lenny on his way to Him.

Yeah, Lord. I know I'm moaning too much, but I do really want to do that. Help him. So I'm praying for Lenny, Lord.

I'm praying for Lenny.

Finally, Josh suggests that we hold another liturgy and souling, just for Lenny this time. Before I can get too excited, he remarks that we don't have any more soul cakes, and we're fasting, so we'll use raisins. And do I want to ask for the prayers this time, since Lenny appeared to me?

Great.

I give one raisin to Josh.

And one to Darryl.

None for me.

Offer it up, Harry.

Yeah. Praying for you, Lenny.

DARRYL

The raisin consumed, I recite the prayer for the dead that I've said so often since last night that I've actually got it memorized, then I try for some silent prayer. Distractions keep floating in.

Harry's not happy, I can tell. This really is in another league from anything we've done at home. Hunters don't do this kind of thing by halves. Josh seems to think it's a totally proportionate response, and I guess considering what happened, he's not wrong.

All the same, the thought of another twenty-four hours or more before we can eat . . .

No, I'm not thinking about that. It will go quickly enough. And there's a guy who got murdered with no time to make things right with God, who's burning—or burning with longing—right now, who for some reason God has singled us out to help.

Lord, I pray for Lenny.

In the chair just behind me, Harry gasps. Nodding off again? I open my eyes to find a figure standing in front of us. Black hair, pale, gashed skin, normal hunter clothes, ragged and blood-stained. Lenny?

The figure's arms are held out just slightly, very loosely, palms open. There's something utterly, overwhelmingly passive about his stance, like he's completely incapable of doing anything, affecting anything, and yet no one could see him without understanding the pleading.

My eyes make out more as they focus. The wounds are savage. Is this how he looked at the moment of his death?

But I'm not afraid. Not even one little bit.

Weird.

And then, perhaps when I blink, the figure is gone.

"Did you see that?" I turn to Josh, but from the way Josh is staring, wide-eyed, at the same spot, I don't need an answer. In fact, considering how Josh had taken all this in stride, I'm startled by the depth of shock on his face.

"*Now* do you believe me?" says Harry, in a martyred tone.

"Which part of *fasting all day* suggested that we didn't believe you?" I snap. But after a moment, I add, "Sorry."

Everyone's short-tempered and *hangry*. Well, not Josh, so much.

Josh rushes to the console, tapping at the screen. Harry and I follow, puzzled.

"Harry, which man did you see?" Josh waves to the photo he's pulled up again.

"*Which?*" Harry shoots him a disbelieving look. "You just saw him too. Here ..." Harry points to the light-skinned, dark-haired figure standing beside the equally dark-haired Thiago. "Him. Lenny Miller."

Josh shakes his head. "That ain't Lenny Miller." He points to another light-skinned guy, the one standing beside West. "*That's* Lenny."

"What?" Harry shoots a confused look at the bone nestled reverently in its little hide-lined box. "But if that's Lenny's bone . . ."

"Mebbe it is or mebbe it ain't Lenny's bone. But the guy ain't Lenny."

"Then . . ." My braid slides forward and brushes the screen as I peer at the five men in the photo—pale Lenny, dark-skinned West, blonde-haired Ed, wiry Thiago, and our ghostly visitor. "Who is he?" But again, it's one of those moments when I know what Josh is going to say.

Josh taps a finger to the familiar stranger. "*That* . . . is Tidna."

HARRY

Tidna?

"Tidna Way? The murderer?" I check.

Josh nods.

"No *way*!" I'm practically shouting.

"Definitely Way," says Josh, apparently still able to joke even after fasting for this long.

"Oh, *haha*! I don't *believe* it!" Harry waves a fist furiously. "We've done all this for the *killer*?"

"I dunno," says Josh. "Our intention were to pray for the soul that visited you. But we've been praying for Lenny by name. So, who will God apply it to?"

"Maybe he'll split it between them?" suggests Darryl.

"But . . . how the heck isn't Tidna in hell?" I demand. "Maybe it is a demon!"

Josh gives me an infuriatingly patient look. "I don't think it's a demon. Why shouldn't Tidna be in purgatory? I reckon he made up with God before he died. I know Thiago said he prayed with him. He just went with a whole loada muck on his soul."

The *murderer*. That foul, rotten, cowardly murderer who didn't even have the guts to do the deed himself!

"Well, that's that, right?" I look from Josh to Darryl. "Let's get a meal together and eat!"

Josh raises an eyebrow. "Why? There's still a soul needs praying for."

I turn to Darryl, but she just shrugs. "At least we have the name right, now."

"What? You two are so . . . so . . . *urgh*!" Fierce anger swamping me, I limp to the cupboard and grab the packet of chocolate cookies we've been saving for All Saints' Day, toss them up into my bunk, and climb up after. "I am not fasting another minute for that killer!" I snarl—then slam the door behind me.

JOSHUA

Darryl and I exchange a rueful look. "Oh well," I say. "Two's better than nothing. D'you wanna take the first prayer watch?" She'll get more sleep that way.

"Okay." She don't argue, definitely paler than usual. Guess farmers just don't fast this much, normally.

I head into my little cab bedroom, but I lie awake for a long time, staring into the darkness.

My one big memory of Lenny and Tidna is a weekend when I were mebbe . . . four? Dad and Uncle Z left me with Technicolor while they went in-city. And Lenny and Tidna turned up for a cookout. West, Thiago, and Ed came down with some'at, couldn't even get outta their sleeping bags come morning. It were summer, so Tidna spent hours down at the stream, helping me make mud animals, while Lenny kept watch.

I guess that's why I remember Tidna better than Lenny. They disappeared from my life soon after, and grown-ups got odd if I mentioned 'em. And it weren't 'til I were older that I found out what had happened. But . . . no one's all bad or all good. Loada ways Tidna coulda kept a little kid from getting et without going to such trouble.

Did Tidna die the same way as Lenny? Is that why he's all clawed up like that? Is it *his* bone? Guess it could be, though I can't explain why to Darryl and Harry without giving secret stuff away. Or mebbe he's wearing Lenny's wounds for some reason. Mebbe it is Lenny's bone, but God—or Tidna?—chose us because we were on this spot.

None of it really matters.

Tidna's right with God—must be, if he's in purgatory. And we can help him.

HARRY

I hold the crinkly packet in my hand, turning it end over end, feeling the shape of the individual cookies inside.

Why haven't I opened it yet? I'm so hungry. And I *refuse* to fast for that vile murderer. Josh and Darryl are totally taking things to extremes.

All the same . . . it's the middle of the night. I can eat the cookies for breakfast. They're the only food I've got, and if those two are going to keep this up until tomorrow night—and I bet they are—I'd rather stay up here out of the way.

Yeah, I'll ration myself. It's a good big pack of cookies. If I just go to sleep now, I can make them last all day.

I should have brought my book reader up, though. What the heck am I gonna do with myself tomorrow?

DARRYL

This All Souls' Day has been a million years long. I sit in my folding seat, too tired and hungry to kneel anymore but still trying to pray. Even Josh has gone quiet now.

Occasionally, we knock on Harry's door and check he's okay, which he confirms monosyllabically. Except for sidling down to answer nature's call a couple of times— silently, no eye contact—he shows no inclination to come out. Still furious with us, I guess—but then, he doesn't need to come out. He's got all those cookies.

Cookies . . .

My aching stomach gnaws at my backbone with fierce fangs. Is this how Lenny felt? And Tidna? Why was *he* all gashed up?

Nah, they had it worse.

Josh said for fasting purposes, the day ends at midnight. We're going to have a meal then, before we go to bed. I check the time again. Three more hours . . .

"D'you think it's really about Tidna?" Josh says, suddenly.

"What do you mean?" My hungry brain feels as white and empty as the snowy landscape as I try to crank it into action.

"I mean, our prayers *will* help Tidna, no question," says Josh. "S'why I won't *ever* stop praying for Dad and Uncle Z. But Tidna's *in*." His gaze darts to the bone. "He's just gotta be . . . whatever the equivalent of *patient* is where there's no time . . . and then he'll be with God. I mean, who knows how long . . . how *much* . . . he's already experienced."

I think of that strange figure, the pleading I sensed. *Was it pleading? Or just . . . a longing so intense, so beyond what we've ever experienced, that it was unrecognizable? What we're doing moves him closer to the Object of his all-consuming longing. So he must be very happy to receive it. But if he doesn't need it-need it, then why are we doing it?*

"So," Josh continues, sounding infuriatingly mentally alert despite having also finally given up kneeling, "this whole Tidna-appearing thing . . . is it more to . . . to test *our* love or . . . or give us the opportunity to love more or . . . something?"

I blink at him, my mind blanker than ever. "But we don't love Tidna."

"Don't we?" Josh stares back at me, his eyebrow rising.

"Love is action."

Love is action? Father Ben says something similar. *Love is doing, not feeling.* Do I love Tidna as, like, a brother soul? Despite what he did? Is that why I'm doing this?

"Anyway, no one's all bad, and he were real sorry," Josh adds.

This conversation is making my energy-deprived brain hurt.

"God is merciful *and* just, right?" I say, hoping to satisfy Josh so he'll stop making me *think*. "So, maybe especially when there's a really big gap between how very sorry a soul is and what a serious lot of, of"—I wave a hand, searching, then use his word—"of *muck* they're stuck with, God shows that soul mercy and lets them seek extra prayers from a person who will *also* be helped by praying for them."

"Reckon so," says Josh. He's silent for a moment, then adds, "But I bet most souls, if God says they can approach someone, don't choose *nowadays* to appear unless they've got a darn good reason like a relative or some tie." He gestures vaguely over his shoulder. "I bet they appear back when everyone knew all about purgatory and knew what to do for them. Don't make no difference to God when they appear, right?"

Attempting to wrap my mind around God's timelessness is even more beyond me than usual. Fortunately, after I make a noise of assent, Josh falls silent.

Lord, please accept all this for Tidna. Josh is right, he can't have been all bad or he wouldn't have been so sorry. And Thiago wouldn't have liked him, either, I guess.

JOSHUA

It's 11:00 p.m. I get the All Saints roast beef from the fridge and put it in the omniprocessor with some veggies—barely resisting the desire to lick the raw meat juices from my fingers—and set it to cook by midnight. That way we can eat as soon as All Souls' Day is over.

I just hope . . .

How will we know if we've done any good? I guess we simply have to trust. And keep praying for Lenny and Tidna, mebbe?

The interCar radio chimes, such an unexpected noise in the utter night silence, here in the middle of nowhere, that I start violently, my heart slamming against my ribs.

Darryl jolts upright in her chair, blinking like she'd nodded off.

"Hello, Wilson 'Vi? I see lights. You still up?" West's familiar, welcome voice blasts from the speaker. "Don't you know better than to let baby rex use your tracks as a chew toy?"

So, they came up right away, regardless of the weather? Why am I not surprised?

I take a few deep breaths to get my shocked heartbeat under control, ambushed by an unexpectedly strong wave of relief—then push the button to reply. "Good timing, Technicolor—we're about to eat dinner."

"*Dinner*? What time zone are you cubs living in up here?"

Soon enough, they're trooping in through our carefully aligned side-doors, carrying their mugs and folding chairs, ready to socialize. West, who sounded cheerful enough before, now looks concerned, his dark face wrinkled up with worry. Blond-haired, pale-skinned, easy-going Ed has his free arm thrown around Thiago's wiry shoulders. And dark-haired, quick-tempered, over-serious Thiago—tousle-headed and rumpled and blinking, like he'd gone to bed already, probably having driven earlier—is crying quietly.

"Thiago?" I hurry to him. "What's wrong? Are you hurt?"

"He came down from his bunk all upset like this, and we ain't got a word outta him yet," says West in an undertone.

Thiago walks straight to the still candle-ringed bone and stares down at it. "Is this Tidna's?"

"Or Lenny's," I say, staring at him. How'd he even know the bone were there?

He gives a big sniff and nods. "Sorry," he says, finally. "I never had a dream quite like what I just had. Lenny were there—I don't really remember anything about where—but he were waiting for someone. And then Tidna came along, running—skipping, really—happy as a fresh hatchling. And Lenny kinda gave him a cuff—you know, *you idiot*, kinda thing. And then they flung an arm around each other's shoulders and ... walked off somewhere. Somewhere ... really good. And I woke up and ... I can't seem to stop crying."

Joy surges inside me. Darryl rises from her chair and

takes a couple of steps, grabbing my hand and Thiago's, her smile lighting up her face.

Guess we do know, after all!

HARRY

I sit up in my bunk, listening hard. Tidna's free? Lenny too? And they've what . . . forgiven and forgotten? 'Cause they're in heaven? Is that what the dream means?

Wow. Just . . . wow. What we did actually made a difference? I guess we can't know that for sure. But it seems that way.

Plates clinking, kitchen noises . . . *Finally!*

"Thiago," Josh is saying, "we have *a lot* to tell you."

I slide open the door and climb down.

"Uh-oh," booms West. "Who's wearing a bad-luck brace?"

"It's only sprained," I say.

I can feel my face going all hot as Darryl and Josh stare at me. At what I hold. I step to the table and set the unopened packet of cookies down in the center.

I've never been so hungry in my life.

But I guess it was worth it, after all.

###

Aspects of this story are based on real events. A lady from the author's church lives in a manor house that has a priest hole dating back to the Elizabethan penal times,

when Catholics were persecuted in Britain. One day, two guests staying in the room with the priest hole woke up in the night to find a figure standing at the end of the bed, staring silently at them. They said that there was nothing at all frightening about the experience, despite the figure's sunken, red-rimmed eyes and general emaciation. When they told the lady who owned the house, she was shocked, because she knew what the couple did not: that during the penal times, a priest had starved to death in the priest hole after the lord of the manor was arrested. The figure described had all the physical symptoms of someone who had died of starvation, and a modern-day priest explained to her that the dead priest's soul was probably seeking prayers from purgatory.

The interesting things about this are:

- The couple both saw the figure, so they weren't asleep.
- Neither of them knew the history of the house or the priest.
- Neither of them found the apparition frightening.

All these things are included in this story.

To find out more about why farm kids Darryl and Harry are living a hunter lifestyle with Joshua, don't miss the first quick-read in the unSPARKed series, *Please Don't Feed the Dinosaurs*.

ABOUT THE AUTHOR

CORINNA TURNER has been writing since she was fourteen and likes strong protagonists with plenty of integrity. Although she spends as much time as possible writing, she cannot keep up with the flow of ideas, for which she offers thanks—and occasional grumbles!—to the Holy Spirit. She is the author of over twenty-five books, including the Carnegie Medal Nominated I Am Margaret series, and her work has been translated into four languages. She was awarded the St. Katherine Drexel award in 2022.

She is a Lay Dominican with an MA in English from Oxford University and lives in the UK. She is a member of a number of organizations, including the Society of Authors, Catholic Teen Books, Catholic Reads, the Angelic Warfare Confraternity, and the Sodality of the Blessed Sacrament. She used to have a Giant African Land Snail, Peter, with a 6½″ long shell, but now makes do with a cactus and a campervan.

To learn more, visit: www.IAmMargaret.com.

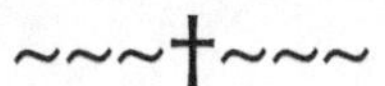

LUCY AND THE FORBIDDEN SECRET

by Antony B. Kolenc

On All Hallows' Day, Sister Dymphna pulls me aside after our *vespers* prayers at early evening, as we make our way to another silent supper. She has mischief in her eyes.

"Lucy," she says in a whisper, pressing a wrinkle from the long, black novice's habit that flows to her boots. "Sister Agnes is up to something again—I'm sure of it."

I've been a novice studying under the Benedictine nuns at Harwood Abbey since November 1185—less than a year. It took me less than a month to realize I shouldn't agree when Dymphna says *anything* about other novices.

"Oh?" I turn away to show her I'm not interested.

The problem is that this tactic never works with Dymphna. She never needs encouragement to imagine Agnes doing wrong. She seems ready to find and announce every rule Agnes breaks each day.

"Aye, Lucy. I feel certain. God has blessed me with a keen sense of intuition, you know."

"So you've said," I reply. She's said it often, after all.

Truth be told, I think Dymphna is envious because Agnes is quite pretty. I'm told that Agnes used to have the most beautiful honey-golden hair at Penwood Manor—that is, until she came to this nunnery and had it shorn off to become a novice.

When I got to this abbey and had my own hair shorn, Agnes already looked like everyone else, with the same white cloth that closely frames our faces and the same white novice veil that covers our hair.

As we head toward the little refectory, Dymphna speaks louder than anyone ought in a nunnery. "I saw her staring at the garden door, Lucy."

"Shh!" I say, as Sister Regina marches past us.

Sister Regina is the kindest nun at Harwood Abbey. I love her like a mother, but the look she shot as she passed was disturbing. Is she angry at me? Disappointed? Upset? She must have heard what Dymphna said. As one of the obedientiaries in charge of us, Sister Regina might need to report us to that grumpy Sister Cecilia. *Then* what?

"Well, Lucy?" Dymphna says, after Sister Regina leaves. "What do you think Sister Agnes is up to?"

I honestly have no idea how to answer. Knowing Agnes, she probably *is* up to some naughtiness. Out of all the novices, Agnes is the one most likely to get in trouble—often because Dymphna pays such close attention and then whispers about it to everyone she sees.

"We should ask the saints to pray for her," I say.

Praying is not Dymphna's strength but, in her defense,

she *did* grow up the pampered daughter of a wealthy land baron. She probably didn't do much praying as a young girl before her parents sent her off to this nunnery to learn discipline under the nuns. I first met her before she became a novice. She went by the name Silvia back then.

"Look! Here comes Sister Monica." Dymphna's smile widens. "Maybe I'll see what *she* thinks about it."

The problem with Dymphna—or should I say *one* of her problems—is that she doesn't seem to care about the sin of detraction. I doubt she knows how horrible 'tis.

But detraction *is* a sin—an enormous one, too. If a person knows something bad about another person, why spread the word around, even if 'tis true? What good does that do? All it does is cause scandal and judgmental thoughts, which leads to others spreading *more* detraction around until the whole lot of us novices are chattering away about each other instead of focusing on our prayers.

"Maybe we should keep our suspicions to ourselves," I say, in the kindest possible way.

Dymphna smiles again. "I suppose that I *can* keep this little secret 'twixt the two of us, Lucy ... but only if you help me figure out what Sister Agnes is doing."

The last thing I want is more rumors going around about Agnes, so I give Dymphna a huff.

"Fine," I say, as we enter the refectory. "After supper."

With today being All Hallows' Day, and also a Sunday, we had an extra-long Mass with the monks of Harwood Abbey this morning to honor all the saints in heaven.

It never ceases to astound me that the saints still care what goes on in this world of ours. They intercede to God for us when we ask them—and I've got plenty of petitions.

After supper, we sit silently in the refectory while Sister Regina leads us in a contemplation on this special feast day. She tells us to remember all the people in this world for whom we want the saints to pray.

I think about Father; I hope he will visit the abbey soon. Maybe Saint Peter can pray for him. I remember my brothers, too: Ralph, Maurice, and Aubrey. And I think about Agnes, of course. When she became a novice, she took the name of Saint Agnes—a virgin and martyr who died for the faith. Maybe *Saint* Agnes can intercede on behalf of *Sister* Agnes to help her stay out of trouble!

Across the refectory, Agnes is praying alone with her eyes shut tight. Why does she look so sad? Is she crying? Dymphna is watching her closely, too.

Finally, we head back to our cells for silent reflection before we gather later for *compline,* our final night prayers.

Agnes walks alone behind us. I can see at a glance that her eyes are red and puffy. Dymphna might be right: something *is* going on, and there's no telling what Agnes could do when she gets upset (which happens a *lot*).

Unfortunately, Agnes never talks about *why* she's upset. Something evil must have happened to her at Penwood Manor before she came to the nunnery. 'Tis some kind of secret, I think. Maybe she'll tell me one day.

"See what I mean?" Dymphna whispers as we walk. "You know her better than the rest of us, Lucy. *Ask* her."

"Shh," I say. We're not supposed to be talking in the halls, and I don't plan on breaking the rules just to satisfy Dymphna's curiosity. "*Later.*"

Later never comes because Sister Regina walks us to our cells. She normally bids me goodnight with a warm smile, but not tonight. She only gives a strange stare and a nod.

Maybe she *is* angry at me. Maybe she thinks that *I'm* the one spreading rumors about Agnes. I hope she doesn't report me to Sister Cecilia. I could be disciplined for a whole year for the sin of detraction.

We shut ourselves in our cells for bedtime. After some time passes, I hear the slow, careful creak of the door opening next to mine—the cell that Agnes sleeps in.

She *is* up to something.

Dymphna's cell is down the hall from us, so she isn't likely to have heard the noise, but what if she *did*? She would start squawking at us like an owl at midnight.

I wait a moment, listening by the edge of my cell for the sound of footsteps. They soon come: the patter of the feet of a novice trying to be careful . . . but not careful enough to be *truly* careful enough, if that makes sense.

When the footsteps disappear around the corner, I open my own cell door—much more carefully, without even a creak. I tiptoe down the hall in bare feet, following the beats of the leather-soled boots belonging to Agnes.

What is she up to, and what should I do about it?

Sure enough, the sounds lead toward the garden door, just as Dymphna suspected. I hate when that girl is right.

The door opens with almost no noise.

"Agnes!" I call out in a whisper—not loud enough.

She's gone, but to where? 'Tis a violation of the rules to go outside after dark, and 'tis a violation of our novice vows to leave the abbey grounds.

Surely, Agnes wouldn't do that, would she?

I crack the door and see her frame heading around the corner of the nunnery. Worst of all, she's taken off her veil. Her shorn hair in the moonlight resembles a cat's back.

"Agnes!" Another failed whisper as she disappears.

Please protect her, Lord.

I don't know where she is heading, but she must be careful going out into the chill air. Stories of the plague scourging Yorkshire have been circulating the abbey for weeks. That illness could mean the death of the poor girl.

But I can't go farther. If I step outside, it would be wrong—plus, I could be disciplined for it. I'll have no choice but to wait and see if she ever returns.

Hours later—who knows how *many* hours—I wake up to a little voice in my head nagging at me to check on Agnes. Surely, she must be back by now, though I didn't hear her creaky door. Then again, I was probably asleep.

That whisper persists in my conscience, like the urging of the Holy Ghost. I've felt it before.

All right, Lord.

I leave my cell and tiptoe toward the garden door. 'Tis unlocked, so perhaps Agnes is still away. An urging to crack it open seeps from my mind to the tips of my fingers, which grasp the handle and pull the door open, just a bit.

I hear speaking near the garden wall: a *man's* voice.

Surely, Brother Leo isn't wandering around the grounds at this hour—especially not around the nunnery. Nay, no monk of Harwood Abbey speaks aloud at this hour.

"You are home safe, my dear," the man says.

"*Fine,*" Agnes says. "You've made your point, Roger. Now let me return to this nunnery in peace."

"I will wait for you, my dear."

"Please *don't,*" she says to him.

The annoyed tone in her voice sounds as if she's about to come inside, so I shut the door and hurry back toward my cell. Soon, the sound of steps echo in my direction.

What should I do? Can I go back to bed and pretend that I've heard and seen nothing this night? If I tell Sister Regina, will I be a detractor like Dymphna? But if I say nothing at all, will I be holding a forbidden secret?

"Lucy!"

Agnes whispers her surprise louder than she ought, and her eyes grow large with alarm, before settling back to the same melancholy they contained earlier.

"What have you done, Agnes? Who was that man?"

She shakes her head. "Do not ask me, Lucy. Do not breathe a word about *any* of this to anyone. Do you hear?"

As she speaks, her hand moves from behind her back. She is holding a sack with a heavy object in it.

"And what is *that?*"

She stares down at the sack a moment. "Not tonight, Lucy. *Please* do not dare ask me anything else tonight."

With that, she pushes past me and slides into her cell, surprisingly quiet for how upset she looks.

As I re-enter my room, another sound comes from down the hall ... from the direction of Dymphna's cell. Has that meddlesome girl heard all that we said?

Oh, Saint Agnes—now what will I do?

In the middle of the dark night, we arise again to the sound of bells for *matins,* our first prayers on this new day.

Agnes refuses to look at me as we head to the chapel, but Dymphna won't keep her eyes off mine. She smiles and nods, as though she knows exactly what Agnes has done, and knows that *I* know it, too. I'm surprised she doesn't ask me about it in the middle of our prayers.

But what will I do when she *does* ask? I cannot lie—that much I know. But if Dymphna has no right to hear about the misdeeds of Agnes, then I cannot say the *truth,* either.

And what about the nuns? Do I tell Sister Regina? When Mother Abbess returns from her business in York, she deserves to know if one of her novices has broken her vows. Do I sin by keeping this all a secret?

Oh, why did I ever leave my cell last night?

As we chant our prayers in Latin, the peace that usually fills my heart is nowhere within. Even after we return to our cells until dawn, I wonder if I will ever rest again.

Nay ... sleep will evade me this night and *every* night until my conscience forces me to do what I ought. Truth be told, I haven't felt fully at peace for weeks. Something is amiss in my spirit, but I don't know what it might be.

When dawn finally comes, we gather in the refectory for morning bread and ale. As usual, we must eat in silence—a practice for which I am *quite* grateful at the moment.

The puffy eyes of Agnes betray even more distress than my own. Does she cry because of that *man*?

Who was he? Someone from Penwood Manor, perhaps. Agnes didn't seem to want his company, so what does *that* mean? Maybe she has a bullying older brother, like mine.

Or is it possible that Agnes is crying only because she got *caught*? Maybe she worries that I will tell Sister Cecilia. Truly I *should* tell that grumpy nun. When a novice breaks a vow, her very soul may be in peril. Perhaps Sister Cecilia could get Agnes to repent of what she has done.

As we head to the chapel for *prime*, Agnes hurries alone to the front of the line, while Dymphna tugs at my habit and guides me to the very end of the line.

"Well?" she says, her eyes smiling more than her lips.

"Well ..." I shrug. "I am disappointed in our dear sister, that much I can say."

The way Dymphna's eyes catch fire, I know I've already said too much. Have I given in to the sin of detraction, too?

"*Tell* me, Lucy."

I fold my arms. "I truly cannot say more, Sister."

She gives me a smirk. "Aye, Sister, you truly *can* say more. We had a bargain; you made a promise."

"I never promised anything!"

She frowns. "Mother Abbess says that our very words are our solemn vows. Yesterday, you agreed that you would find out what Sister Agnes is up to, and now you must fulfill that promise because—"

"Shh!"

Sister Regina is standing quite still at the corner of the hallway heading to the chapel. She is staring at me once more. She may have overheard our conversation again.

"Good dawning, Sister Regina," I say as I pass by.

She barely gives me a nod in return, turning and hurrying down the hallway in the other direction.

Why is she so angry with me?

My conscience accuses me for keeping this secret as long as I have already. Sister Regina has a way of always knowing the truth. She *must* know what happened.

Dymphna draws close to my ear. "If you don't tell me about Sister Agnes, I will have no choice but to tell Sister Cecilia what I heard last night. Think about *that*, Lucy, and let me know your final decision by *vespers* this evening."

That girl seems to relish in one detraction after another. And she has given me a reprieve of only hours to meditate on what is the right and good thing to do.

After our *terce* prayers, we do chores. Through God's grace, Agnes and I are part of a group of novices assigned to clear dead leaves from the garden on this chill day.

As we pick the crusty brown leaves from the dormant flower bed, Agnes works her way toward me. At last, she must be ready to talk about last night.

I gesture for her to draw nearer. "Agnes, you know that I am your dear friend, as well as your sister in Christ."

She stands beside me and starts to tear. "'Tis not what

you think." She wipes her cheek on her black habit sleeve.

I put my hand on her back and rub it gently. "You cannot possibly know what I'm thinking, now can you?"

She nods. "You think I left the abbey grounds for *him*."

Maybe she *does* know what I think. "Well, you *did* risk leaving the abbey—even with that plague about. And then you returned in the company of that man. Who was he?"

"Do you know what day today is, Lucy?"

"'Tis Monday."

She sighs. "Today is also the day of All Souls."

"Aye—that, too."

Like many monasteries, Harwood Abbey marks the day of All Souls immediately after the Feast of All Hallows— no longer in October. We remember the souls who went before us, enduring the cleansing fires of purgatory.

Agnes bows her head. "My mum died five years ago on this day. Did you know that?"

Is that why she is so sad, Lord?

Too many of us have lost our mothers. Mine died after I was born. I can't even remember the color of her eyes. Father talks of her all the time, though. He loved her so.

"I'm sorry for you, Agnes . . . but what does this have to do with that man? And why break your vows by leaving?"

Just then, Dymphna pops out the garden door with a skip and a grin. "*There* you two are!"

Agnes pales. "What did you *do*, Lucy?"

"Whatever are you two speaking about?" Dymphna says, all too innocently. "I want to know, too."

The cheeks on Agnes change from pale to pink; her eyes

flash hot. "This doesn't involve you, Dymphna. Why must you always seek out the *bad*? Leave us alone!"

Dymphna folds her arms tight, like a constricting snake. "Don't blame me for your selfishness, Sister Agnes. If you followed the rules, you wouldn't be in so much trouble."

With a grunt, Agnes storms inside. Whatever she wanted to tell me will need to wait until later.

"Can you believe the boldness of that girl?" Dymphna says. "Now, Lucy—'tis time you told me the whole story."

But I cannot tell her *any* of the story, can I? Agnes is right. What business is this of Dymphna . . . or of *mine*? I should just forget the whole affair.

I turn to leave. "I have nothing else to say. I'm sorry."

As I march off, I can feel her eyes staring nasty holes in my white-veiled head. If she reports me to Sister Cecilia, so be it. I will *not* sin by more detraction on this holy day.

God will make it right in the end.

After we finish our second meal, I go back to my cell for more rest and reflection. When the bells ring again, I return to the hallway for our afternoon lessons.

"Sister Lucy?" Agnes is waiting for me there, holding the heavy sack from last night like a weapon.

I want to be a better friend to her now than I was earlier when I gave in to the sin of detraction. "How can I help?"

She pauses, her eyes tearing up again. "There is something I really must tell you, but I—I don't know how to say it. It has to do with what you saw last night."

I supposed as much. Maybe her conscience has brought

her to this moment of confession, but suddenly I'm unsure that I should be the one to hear about these sins of hers.

"Are you sure 'tis *me* you should tell? Wouldn't it be best to speak with a priest, or maybe Sister Regina? None of this is my affair, after all."

"That's where you're so very wrong, Lucy. You see—"

Just then, Sister Cecilia lumbers toward us as if she is going on Crusade. She's so tall, most novices refer to her as *Sister Treetop*. Her hands swing wildly at her sides.

"I wonder what *she's* up to," I say.

Agnes reels back as the nun halts before us and points her huge fingers in our faces. "You—both of you—come with me. There's something we need to discuss . . . *now*."

Sister Cecilia escorts us to the room with the large table, where the obedientiaries meet to make their decisions.

Sister Regina is waiting there, her eyes bowed as low as her spirits seem. Less surprising, Dymphna stands in a corner, her arms still folded and her lips pursed in a smirk.

Sister Cecilia clears her throat and straightens her posture, towering over us even more than usual. "We have received a . . . a *report* . . . that the two of you were out of your cells last night, and that at least one of you may have left the sacred walls of this nunnery."

I bow my head as low as Sister Regina's and wait for Agnes to say something. This is *her* secret to tell, after all.

But when Agnes starts to speak, the nuns seem shocked by her defiant tone—as am I.

"Why haven't you told her yet?" Agnes says to them, as

harsh as can be.

Sister Cecilia takes a moment to recover. "*What* did you say to me, novice? How dare you take that tone!"

As the tears pool up in her eyes, Agnes addresses Sister Regina in a more pleading voice. "Why keep this secret from her? 'Tis a cruel way to treat someone you love!"

Sister Regina's reddening face turns to me. Our eyes lock, and suddenly the reality is clear for everyone to see.

They're talking about me . . .

Sister Cecilia opens her mouth—probably to scream at Agnes—but Sister Regina raises a hand to keep the peace.

"Patience, Sister," she whispers. "The girl speaks truth."

The expression on my face must be as confused as the thoughts swirling through my scattered mind. Dymphna's startled eyes show that she is as baffled as I am.

"W-what are you *talking* about?" I say. "What secret?"

Sister Cecilia's face is redder than Sister Regina's now, but it has a new expression I've never seen on it: *doubt*. That grumpy nun doesn't know what to say for once.

When Sister Regina cannot answer immediately, Agnes bursts into tears. "You want to know why I left the abbey last night, Lucy? *Do* you? I did it for *your* sake."

Her sputtering words hit me like a charging boar. "For me?" My voice is trembling now. "But . . . but why?"

Agnes swings her sack on the table and reaches inside. She pulls out a thick beeswax candle set in a wooden holder intricately carved with images of kneeling angels.

"A prayer candle?" I say.

She nods. "My father gave me this candle after my mum

died. He told me that if I lit it and prayed for her on the day of All Souls, then my mum's soul would be released from the fires of purgatory into the glories of heaven."

Poor Agnes—from what I've learned, that's not how purgatory works at all. "'Tis a beautiful candle, Sister Agnes, but . . . I-I still don't understand."

Agnes wipes the tears on her sleeve, her composure returning for a moment. "I went home to Penwood Manor last night to fetch this candle for *you*, Lucy."

Why I would need such a candle is still a deep mystery, even if it *could* help a soul escape the fires of purgatory.

"You went to Penwood last night?" Sister Cecilia says, finally finding her voice—her *reprimanding* voice, that is.

Agnes starts weeping again. "I needed to get this candle for Lucy! I know it was foolish, but I just couldn't think what else to do . . . how else I could help her!"

Now, I am more confused than ever, but before I can say another word, Dymphna bursts into the conversation.

"Is that *really* why you went there, Sister Agnes? Or did you go to see that *man*?"

The two nuns stare in disbelief. Dymphna definitely overheard what we said in the hallway last night.

"You were with a . . . *man* last night?" Sister Regina says.

Agnes shakes her head. "Not like *that*. This man— Roger—has pursued me for some time. When he saw me at Penwood last night, he followed me back here."

Dymphna folds her arms. "You expect them to believe that you have no interest in that man at all?"

Agnes plops onto the bench. "I *don't!* In fact—if you must know—I am *already* engaged, should my dear Lawrence ever return from Crusade in the Holy Land."

Sister Cecilia steadies herself on the table. "Engaged . . . to be married? Yet you took a novice's vows, you lying *snake*? You came to this nunnery under false pretenses!"

Agnes sobs into her hands. "I needed to escape this Roger. I'm sorry for deceiving you, Sister! I see now how *horrid* it is, what I have done. Can you ever forgive me?"

Sister Cecilia shows no mercy. "*Nay!* Mother Abbess shall *expel* you from this nunnery, Agnes—actually, we will use your given name from now on: Muriel."

Muriel must be the name Agnes was given at her baptism.

"Enough about *whatever* her name is," Dymphna says. "What is this secret about *Lucy*? Why does no one tell it?"

Agnes-Muriel buries her face into her black sleeves. There will be no secrets coming from *her* anytime soon.

I turn to Sister Regina, whose cheeks also are streaming with tears. "What is it that no one is telling me, Sister?"

She cannot even look at me. "We did not mean to hurt you, Lucy. We found out ourselves only yesterday. Sister Cecilia felt it would be best if Mother Abbess told you the news herself when she returns on the morrow from York. But Agnes—*Muriel*—has made that impossible now."

Muriel lifts her head from her arms. "I saw a messenger arrive yesterday morn. I thought perhaps there was news from Penwood Manor—maybe about my dear Lawrence. I should never have spied on what he told Sister Cecilia."

"*What* did he tell Sister Cecilia?" I say.

Sister Regina places her arms around my shoulders in a soothing way, but why is she comforting me like this?

"The messenger arrived with news from your manor. The plague spreading across the shire has hit your home, Lucy. Your brothers took ill weeks ago . . . your father, also."

I falter for a moment. "Are . . . are they all well?"

Sister Regina holds me tighter. "We are told that your brothers are recovering, but . . . your father—he . . . he was not as strong as they. I—I am sorry, Lucy . . . so *truly* sorry."

"Father . . . Are you saying that my father is *dead*?"

I cannot believe the words I am speaking. Father was so strong and healthy a few months ago when I last saw him.

Please, Lord—let this be a nightmare from which I can wake!

"Aye," Sister Regina says softly. "With the plague, they were forced to bury him last month, with so many of the others who have perished during this hard, dreary time."

I stare at the cold stone wall and then turn to Sister Regina. "Is that why you haven't been speaking to me? Is that why you hurry away every time I draw near?"

Sister Regina's eyes are as sorrowful as I've ever known them. "I could barely see you without my heart breaking."

Muriel pushes the prayer candle toward me. "That's why I went to Penwood to get this for you. If you light this candle for your father today—this day of All Souls—his spirit *must* be released into the glories of heaven."

Is it true that we can so easily free the souls of those we have lost: Muriel's mother . . . my father?

Sister Cecilia shakes her head. "Muriel, you *foolish* girl, that is only a superstition. Of course, we can pray for the souls in purgatory, but lighting this candle gives no special guarantee to free a soul from the cleansing fires."

I look to Muriel, who seems to have risked all she had at this nunnery on nothing but a superstition. "I'm so sorry, Muriel. Your kindness toward me has cost you greatly."

Sister Cecilia nods. "'Tis her *foolishness* and lies that have cost her everything."

Muriel embraces me. "Perhaps I *am* a fool, Lucy. But I thank God now that my secret is finally revealed, for the venom of these lies has been poisoning my very soul."

Father is dead. How could I not know it?

Perhaps that is why my spirit has felt so amiss these past weeks. Did I sense the trouble plaguing my family?

But I never had the chance to tell Father goodbye . . . to tell him how much I loved him . . . how much I appreciated all he did to raise me up to be the person I am today.

He raised me alone . . . without Mother to help him know how to speak to such a stubborn girl as I, with so many questions and such a silly nature.

And now he's gone . . . forever—or maybe *not* forever.

I stare at the candle burning in my cell—the one Muriel gave me for the day of All Souls. I make the sign of the cross and kneel before the crucifix of my dying Lord.

"Dear Jesus, you are no stranger to suffering, I know. Please watch over the souls of Father and Mother—and Muriel's

mother, also. Let our souls be reunited with theirs one day in heaven. And take their souls to your side as soon as you possibly can. Forgive them for their transgressions in this life."

Even with forgiveness, though, our sins cost us a price. That is clear now, especially to Muriel. But she is not the only one to feel discipline for her wrongdoings.

For her detractions against Muriel, Dymphna has also been punished. Perhaps she had her reasons for spreading news of everyone else's sins. Maybe by keeping the focus on the sins of others, she hoped to hide her own faults.

But we all have our faults. Aye, if we spent more time rooting out our own sins instead of worrying about the sins of others, this world would be a holier place, I'm sure.

As for my own sins, Sister Cecilia assures me that—dead father or not—I shall be punished for an entire year for my role in keeping Muriel's violations a secret. I should have reported her immediately to Sister Cecilia once I knew that she had broken her novice vows.

I know in my heart that Sister Cecilia is right about that.

The sun is shining again today . . . finally.

I sit on the garden wall and remember times gone by, when the spring flowers bloomed so purple and yellow and red as berries. Those were good days, sitting with Sister Regina and my friend Xan, before he left for Lincoln.

The sound of younger girls playing with their dolls rises from the path out front. Maud's voice is loudest of all. Ever since I became a novice, I haven't spent much time with that poor girl, who was like a little sister to me. I think

Maud is angry about that, but there's nothing I can do.

Rules must govern the lives of us novices or else we will all fall into a pit together. The rules keep us on the path.

The door creaks open: Dymphna. She looks in all directions, as if to ensure no one else will hear her words.

Please, Lord, may she not be here with some story about Sister Monica or another nasty complaint about Sister Cecilia.

"Lucy?" Her voice is gentle as she approaches.

"I'm just enjoying the chill air … and this glorious sun."

She halts before me. "I—I just wanted to—to tell you again how sorry I am about your father … and to apologize for the nasty way I treated you. Can you ever forgive me?"

Maybe the nuns' discipline is already starting to make its mark on her heart.

I smile at her. "Of course I can."

She seems relieved. "With Muriel gone, I think you're my only friend in this place now."

Her words make me feel pity for her because I'm not much of a friend, am I?

I offer her a smile. "Let's try to be the kind of friends who help each other be better people."

The door opens again, and Sister Regina steps into the garden. At her presence, Dymphna gives me a nod and then hurries back inside, greeting the nun as she passes.

"I've been looking for you," Sister Regina says to me.

"I'm here—praying and reflecting."

"I bring good news. I've convinced Mother Abbess to

pardon your punishments on the very day of Easter next year, when we all will end our Lenten penances."

"Thank you, Sister. That was kind of you."

If not for that mercy, I'd be serving out my extra chores and prayers of contrition all through the joyous months of spring and summer, too.

"You know, Lucy, when I first became a novice, I made so many mistakes that Mother Abbess threatened to change my name to Sister *Repenta*."

I shake my head. "You must be jesting."

"Not even a little. 'Tis not easy to mold our hard natures to be soft clay in our Lord's hands. It takes time and prayer and allowing the Holy Ghost to work in us."

"I only wish the clay in my heart wasn't so dry."

Dry clay makes it tough to work within us, doesn't it, Lord?

She draws closer and takes my hand. "I want you to know that I think you're the most promising novice I've ever seen here, Lucy. Do not let your mistakes haunt you, for all of us are sinners at heart, falling short of the glory of God far oftener than we'd care to admit."

I smile and squeeze her warm fingers.

"So," she says. "You keep up with your prayers and your reflecting. For I think that God is working something special in you that—when 'tis finally revealed—will be a marvel to us all."

My warm cheeks don't relish such praise as all that. All I can do is bow my head and nod and offer my own jest.

"I suppose I'll have plenty of time to figure all that out while I'm doing all those extra penances for the next few months."

She laughs. "That you will, Lucy. That you will."

###

If you enjoyed this story, be sure to check out *The Harwood Mysteries* **by Loyola Press. Lucy is a main character in that series, where she and her friends, Xan and Christina, solve suspenseful mysteries at Harwood Abbey and beyond. There are six books in the now-complete series:** *Shadow in the Dark,* *The Haunted Cathedral,* *The Fire of Eden, The Merchant's Curse, Murder at Penwood Manor,* **and** *The Devil's Ransom.* **The short story in this anthology takes place shortly before the events in book five,** *Murder at Penwood Manor.*

ABOUT THE AUTHOR

ANTONY BARONE KOLENC is the author of *The Harwood Mysteries*, the award-winning historical-fiction series for youth published by Loyola Press, as well as other published novels for youth and adults. He notes that the discipline of nuns and clergy in the Middle Ages was much more severe than in modern times, as Lucy and the other novices discover in this short story.

Tony is a long-time member of the Catholic Writers Guild. He retired as a Lieutenant Colonel from the U.S. Air Force Judge Advocate General's Corps after 21 years of military service. A law professor at Ave Maria School of Law, he has also had his non-fiction works published in numerous journals and magazines. He speaks at legal, writing, and home-education events. He and his wife, Alisa, are blessed with many wonderful children and grandchildren.

To learn more about his writings and activities, visit AntonyKolenc.com/.

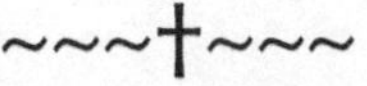

5

HELPLESS

by Theresa Linden

Clouds shifted in front of the moon, and the dark of night swallowed up everything but the closest tombstones. Bare branches whispered in the wind, the unfriendly trees at the back of the graveyard making their presence felt. Vanessa shivered.

The chilly air carried the faint scent of burning wood, probably from a bonfire behind one of the few houses in this part of town. One of those neighbors likely knew the answer to the mystery Vanessa and her friends had come to solve. Granted, the houses were not nearby. The cemetery covered several acres, a good stretch of flat land off the main road, sloping down to gently rising knolls on one side and deep woods at the back.

Dawn and Hattie whispered back and forth behind Vanessa, Hattie's tone insistent and Dawn's sheepish.

Vanessa walked a few yards ahead of them, beside the paved lane that wound through the cemetery. The blades of grass were like icy knives beneath her steps.

Icy knives? Get a grip. It wasn't that cold. If the sun

hadn't set an hour ago, they'd probably see their breath, but it certainly wasn't cold enough to freeze the grass.

And if they were like knives, they'd be slicing the soles of her combat boots and interfering with the confident stride she'd perfected over the past year. Besides, walking on knives would make a lot more noise. She could barely hear her own steps, much less the steps of her friends.

Hattie had talked her and Dawn into this ridiculous venture, investigating the strange lights that everyone was talking about. Dawn had at first refused. Though a bit cautious, or maybe insecure, she always caved in and went along with Hattie's ideas. Kids at school had dared them to check it out after dark, on Halloween night, of course.

Hattie never turned down a dare. She'd even come in costume, wearing an old, oversized jacket and jeans—clothes she'd picked up from the secondhand store, ripped, stained, and decorated with leaves, twigs, and debris. To complete the look, she'd smeared pale gray paint on her face and in her short pixie-style hair—which now stood up in tufts—added some black for sunken cheeks and eyes, and *voilà*: zombie.

Dawn's blue parka hid whatever costume she wore underneath. She'd weaved straw into her long brown hair and smeared makeup from eyes to cheeks, making her look sort of like a raccoon but not at all like a zombie. She didn't watch horror movies. Maybe she wasn't sure what a zombie should look like.

No way was Vanessa dressing as a zombie for a trip to a cemetery. She wore her typical jeans, hoodie, and long denim jacket.

"Let's turn here and walk between gravestones," Hattie whispered, an eager edge to her voice.

"Where exactly were the lights seen?" Vanessa whispered back. She didn't like how the chill in the air made her sound breathless. She was not afraid, not really, although she could totally relate to Dawn's cautious nature. But she didn't want people to think of her that way, so she worked hard to come across as fearless and self-sufficient, the way Hattie did.

"Not sure," Hattie said. "I guess people saw them from the main road. Could've come from anywhere back here."

A soft thump and grunt came from Dawn. "I can't see where I'm walking. Why can't we use the flashlights on our phones?"

"No flashlights," Hattie whispered. "We'll use our phones to get pictures, but until we see anything, we don't want them to know we're out here."

"Who do you mean by *them*?" Vanessa asked. Maybe other teens messing around in the cemetery. Not ghosts. She didn't believe in ghosts. Or witches. Or the undead. She didn't believe in anything magical or supernatural, regardless of the spooky stories kids were now spreading about the strange lights in the cemetery.

"That's what we're here to find out," Hattie said.

With her next step, Vanessa's long jacket brushed something . . . a tombstone not in line with the others. The ground felt different here, more like loose dirt than grass. A recent burial?

Feelings of remorse stirred. Grandpa had died a few weeks ago. They'd buried him somewhere in this big, old cemetery. Right in this area west of the parking lot, if she remembered correctly.

She missed him. She'd hardly visited him at all in the last year of his life. She'd hated seeing him so helpless.

"Oh!" Dawn said, walking a few feet behind Vanessa, maybe bumping into the same tombstone.

Pushing thoughts of Grandpa aside, Vanessa peered into the darkness before and around her. "What did they say the lights looked like? What makes them so strange?"

She shifted her gaze, wanting to look farther. "Maybe they came from one of the houses bordering the cemetery. Maybe someone put up string lights for Halloween or something." That idea made the most sense. With the trees all bare, maybe they could spot a porch light from here. Then they could get out of here and go get pizza—the reason Hattie had given her parents when asking to use their car.

A memory of Grandpa came to Vanessa's mind, possibly triggered by the fresh grave. Grandpa walking toward her with his easy, strolling gait, his kind smile, and gaze lost in the past. After the funeral, she'd seen him in a dream, walking toward her, seeming to climb a hill but making little progress. Looking directly at her with intentional, not distant, eyes. Eyes desperate to communicate something. Then distress changed his face, and he reached for her. He needed her help.

Not wanting to think more about it, Vanessa shook her

head. The dream had felt so real, but Grandpa didn't need her. Not anymore. He might've needed her in the last year of his life, needed to know she cared.

But at his funeral, the minister had said Grandpa was now in heaven. No more suffering, just eternal happiness with Jesus. Not that she believed the minister. She didn't believe in any of that supernatural stuff. Couldn't be proved. People lived. People died. Game over.

The temperature seemed to suddenly drop a few degrees. Vanessa shivered and tried to slide her jacket's top button into the buttonhole. Her gloves made it difficult. She gave up.

"Maybe we're on the wrong side of the cemetery," she said over her shoulder.

Hattie made no reply. Neither did Dawn.

Now that she thought about it, she hadn't heard the slightest stirring behind her for a minute or so.

Vanessa stopped and turned around. She peered into the darkness. "Hattie? Dawn?"

Her skin prickled, as if she stood on the edge of a rooftop. A hint of fear shimmied down her spine. And familiar feelings of helplessness surfaced.

Her friends were gone. She was alone. Could they have gone off in a different direction? Could something have happened to them? Was someone else out here?

"Hattie? Dawn?" she called, looking about as she stuffed a gloved hand into her pocket for her phone.

The phone dropped to the ground.

Heart pummeling against her ribs, jacket now too hot,

she peeled her gloves off and bent down to pat down the cold grass for her phone. Was someone watching her? Some*thing*?

As she stood, she tapped her phone to get some light.

Hot air—a breath?—swept across the back of her neck.

Unable to speak or utter a sound, Vanessa spun to face—

"Ah!" Hattie shouted and grabbed Vanessa's shoulders. The blueish light from Vanessa's phone held under her painted face gave her a half-crazed look. She looked more like a lunatic than a zombie.

Dawn shouted too, but she didn't jump into Vanessa's space. She and Hattie burst out laughing, the teasing but joyful noise driving back phantoms and senseless fears that lurked in cemeteries when teenage girls came out at night on dares.

Vanessa exhaled, relief surging through her. "You freaks!" She punched Hattie's shoulder and shoved her back. Then she laughed too, even as anger at their little betrayal surfaced. The anger shifted to herself. She'd felt so vulnerable and helpless.

Dawn's laughter stopped suddenly. Her eyes opened wide, the dark streaky makeup emphasizing the whites. "What's that?" She pointed.

On the far side of the cemetery, the old side that no one used anymore, little flickering lights appeared. They formed a line that expanded and moved, snaking slowly among the tombstones. It almost reminded Vanessa of headlights on a distant road. But no road ran back there, and cars had two headlights, not one each. And the smaller size didn't work for that theory. And the colors . . . white, yellowish, pale blue, pinkish . . .

"Quick! Take a picture." Hattie brought her phone up.

Dawn did too. Then she and Hattie let out horror movie screams, followed by laughter.

"Let's get out of here!" Dawn turned on her phone's flashlight and ran. Hattie ran with her.

Vanessa couldn't move. She held her phone up but couldn't tear her eyes away from the strange lights to actually take a picture. What were they? No other car had pulled into the cemetery after they had. They would've seen it.

Curiosity urged her to investigate. There had to be a logical explanation. Could she talk her friends into going with her?

Hattie's and Dawn's cheerful voices carried, even though skeletal trees blocked the view of the parking area.

But between their words, the wind carried another sound. A solemn sound. Barely detectable. Maybe voices intoning words together.

"Come on, Nessa!" Hattie shouted. "Let's get pizza."

Two nights later, Vanessa rode her bike down the paved cemetery lane, her bike's headlight turning the weathered asphalt bone gray. She crossed the parking area, heading toward a cherry blossom tree with branches that looked like arms with knobby fingers reaching to the sky. An evergreen shrub grew near it, just big enough to hide her bike.

Moonlight bathed the land, revealing neat rows of newer gravestones and a few older ones at odd angles. The odor of something burning carried on the air. Not wood. Something acrid and unnatural.

Vanessa shut off the headlight, set the kickstand, and hopped off her bike. The warmer weather made her gloves unnecessary, so she tucked them away and grabbed her flashlight, a good one that provided more light than her phone would. Then she took a deep breath, preparing herself. Was she really doing this? All alone?

On her way back to Hattie's car two nights ago, she'd known she would return. No one else seemed willing to actually investigate—not even daredevil Hattie. Cemeteries made people uncomfortable in the daylight and scared people at night. But Vanessa had to know.

Vanessa shone the beam of the flashlight in every direction. Empty parking area. Three barren trees nearby. Cold dead grass beyond them. And rows of headstones in the moonlight.

And somewhere out there lay Grandpa's tomb. Her heart sank with the heaviness of remorse. She hadn't been much of a granddaughter to him in his last year, but she could at least see that no one bothered his burial grounds.

Shining light on the nearest headstones, Vanessa chose her path. They'd seen the lights in the old section, so that's where she headed. She strode with purpose and determination. Not afraid. Not messing around.

It wasn't just remorse that drove her. When her friends

had played that trick on her, making her think she was all alone—or worse, alone with evil breathing down her neck—feelings of helplessness had overcome her. She had become a little girl again, unable to keep up with her older brothers in the woods, separated from them, terrified that she'd never find them. Alone. Afraid. Helpless.

Needy Nessa her brothers used to call her. It wasn't her fault that Mom had babied her or that she'd been the last to learn to tie shoes and work a zipper and ride a bike.

Vanessa gripped the flashlight tighter as she strode over the dead grass. She hated feeling afraid. Helpless. Needy. She didn't want to need anyone but herself. She could do this.

At the back of the new section, the ground sloped down. Old gravestones rose up from less tidy grass in random order and spacing, markers of unique shapes and different sizes, some simply slabs of stone, others intricately carved. A mishmash of styles from generations past. All of them weathered and forgotten.

Further down the slope, mist gathered. It seemed to creep up from the wooded area, which descended even more. Maybe a river or pond was down there too, the warmer weather creating the eerie effect. No sign of strange lights though. Would they still be visible through the mist?

She'd come all this way, might as well investigate a little farther.

Weaving her way around the jumbled array of headstones and grave markers, her flashlight found the figure of an angel. Eyes down, nose missing, it knelt with upturned hands beside a headstone, pleading for a blessing on behalf of the one buried there. Years of wind and rain had eroded the name and dates on the headstone. Born. Died. Remembered only by the angel with no nose.

Ready to move on, Vanessa shifted the beam of the flashlight away, but as the angel's face registered in her mind, she swung back. The eyes weren't looking down. They were looking out. At her.

Weathering had softened the details, but now that she really studied it . . . yes, the angel looked at her through pleading eyes.

She stepped backward, vaguely aware that she would likely bump into something, but she no longer wanted to be here.

The temperature seemed to drop a few degrees.

A chill slithered around her neck and down her spine, the way it had when her friends had abandoned her.

Spinning around, shining the light every which way, she glimpsed only headstones and their shadows. They looked different from when she'd approached this way. Of course they would. She was now viewing them from a different angle.

Having come partway down the sloped ground of the old section, she could see no more of the newer section than the silhouettes of a few tall headstones.

She should go back. Get on her bike and go home. What was she doing out here anyway? Trying to catch the kids with the strange lights? What would she do once she found them? Tell them to go? They were probably playing some game that led up to Halloween night, so they wouldn't even be out here tonight. It was already two days into November.

Vanessa decided upon the easiest path back to the newer section and took a step.

But as her boot swished in the grass, another sound traveled to her from behind: soft, solemn voices intoning words together.

She shut off the flashlight, not wanting to be seen, stuffed it into a jacket pocket, and turned around.

A little golden light appeared a good stone's throw away, the mist giving it a big halo. Then another light in a slightly different color, and another. Moving. Flickering. And then gone.

Heart thumping, Vanessa found herself walking toward the lights, stepping carefully, glancing down to avoid bumping into headstones, peering out to spot the lights again. She didn't dare turn the flashlight back on.

The voices moved away. Or maybe the wind had picked up, increasing the swish and creak of bare branches rubbing together, obscuring the sound of the voices.

Leaves crunched under her boots. She was closer to the woods than she realized. Was she moving toward or away from the lights?

With her next step, flickering yellowish light became visible in a different direction. It seemed much farther away, and it didn't travel like the strange lights appeared to do. Was it a bonfire on a distant property?

The wind died down, and the voices became audible again. Were they off to her left? Behind her?

Resisting the urge to use her flashlight, Vanessa turned toward the sound. Or did she? She saw no lights. *Oh wait* . . . Something glistened in the distance but much lower than the lights had been previously.

She moved toward it, stepping as carefully as she could through the taller grass and steeper slope of the ground.

Moonlight filtered through bare branches above, softly illuminating nearby gravestones and monuments, odd-shaped things. One seemed to grow at an angle out of the leaf-covered ground. Another had toppled, breaking into two large pieces that lay abandoned. More toppled ones. Forgotten ones.

The sight saddened her. Why didn't anyone take care of this part of the cemetery? Why had bodies been buried on the side of a hill anyway?

Continuing down, her boot caught in something. Tall grass? A vine? Momentum had her hastily descending a few more feet, crunching leaves, making too much noise until she steadied herself on a thin tree trunk.

She couldn't see the glimmer of light anymore. Trees and gravestones might've blocked her view. Or maybe *they* shut off their lights because they saw or heard her coming. It was stupid for a girl to come out here alone at night. Why hadn't she thought to bring her pepper spray?

Not wanting them to find her before she found them, Vanessa remained still, held her breath, and listened.

Wind whistled and sighed through branches and insects

sang their high-pitched songs, but a lower sound came to her too. Or was it her imagination? Did it come from above? Maybe even from the newer part of the cemetery?

She took a slow breath, still listening but also wanting to calm herself. Her heart hammered as if lodged in her throat. If the others had moved to the new area, the mist wouldn't hide them.

Turning to make her way back up, Vanessa stepped into shadows and met a dip in the ground. One boot landed awkwardly at a much lower level—throwing her off balance.

She hit the ground sliding, her stomach lurching. Sliding down feet first. Until one foot cracked into something solid lower on the slope.

And icy fingers sliced upward on her calf.

A burst of pain shot up her leg. Duller pain enveloped her entire backside. Her heart raced out of control.

Lying still for a moment, her back to the cold, damp ground, Vanessa squeezed her eyes shut and tried to catch her breath. She willed herself to ride out the pain and get a grip. Then she opened her eyes.

The moon hung above, peeking through the mist and a web of bare branches. A tilted gravestone stood beside her.

Wanting back on her feet—now!—Vanessa lifted her head and shoulders and pushed her elbows into the ground.

Pain shot through her leg before she could push herself up more than a few inches. She flopped back down. Stuck.

After giving the pain a moment to subside, she eased

herself up for a better look at what held her. Seeing her predicament, she groaned and lay back down.

She'd lodged one leg, midway up her calf, between blocks of a toppled tombstone. Or maybe the blocks had come from several old monuments that time and gravity had brought to this one point on the sloped ground. And to which gravity had now brought her.

"Okay, okay," she whispered, "you can handle this." She took a few deep breaths, then pushed herself up as high as she could, to just before the pain became unbearable. And she reached.

Her hand came nowhere near the stones. She flopped back down.

A few breaths later, once the pain lessened, she used her other foot to push against the entrapping stones. They didn't budge.

With a whimper, she lay back down and returned her gaze to the hazy moon.

"What do I do now?" Vanessa whispered to the moon, even as her thoughts turned to her phone. She'd have to call someone for help.

At the thought of calling home, she could almost hear her brothers' chanting, *Needy Nessa needs some help*. Of course, they wouldn't say that to her now. Not at their ages. But somewhere inside, they'd all be thinking it. They'd ask why she had come out here alone. *Needy Nessa can't take care of herself.*

No, she didn't need them. With renewed zeal, Vanessa braced herself and shoved her foot against the topmost block. It didn't budge. She pulled her foot up and slammed it hard, again and again, making the slightest gritty scraping sounds, until the pain brought little points of light to her eyes.

The blocks remained securely in place.

She rested her head back for a moment. Then with a sigh, she reached for her jacket pocket. If she just had a little help . . . but she didn't need to call home. Hattie could probably borrow her parents' car. Hattie might tease her at first, until she realized just how much trouble Vanessa had gotten herself into. But Hattie would help her, and they'd laugh about it one day in the future.

Vanessa's hand slid into an entirely empty pocket.

"Oh no," she whispered with a rush of despair. Her other pocket was empty too. Both the flashlight and the phone must've fallen out.

The cold from the ground seeped through her jacket and jeans, and she shivered. No one even knew she'd come out here tonight. She'd told Mom she was just taking a bike ride.

Someone might spot her bike tomorrow . . . hidden behind that evergreen shrub. Would they think about looking for her?

On the other hand, no one might notice her bike for days. Meanwhile, she'd be stuck down here, in the wild part of the cemetery. Alone.

She broke out in a cool sweat. She was going to die here, freeze to death or dehydrate. The cemetery landscapers would toss old branches down here in the spring and glimpse something not quite right. It would be her dead body, leg still wedged between stone blocks. What would she look like after seven months of decomposing?

Vanessa moaned. *Get a grip! Start thinking of a solution.*

She forced herself up a few inches and peered over her shoulder. Maybe her phone had fallen somewhere nearby.

Moonlight revealed a few gravestones, fallen branches, and patches of leaf-covered earth between bigger sections of misty shadows. She'd have to wait for morning and sunlight to find her phone. Then maybe she could also find a branch long enough to reach it. In the morning . . .

When would her family start worrying about her? They'd be glad to hear her voice once she reached her phone. In the morning. They'd come at once to rescue her.

She could wait. She'd be okay.

With an exhale, she began to ease her head back down.

A familiar sound made her stop, push herself back up on her elbows to just before it hurt too badly, and look around.

It was her phone's ringtone!

Listening intently, she turned toward the sound and shifted her gaze wildly until she spotted . . . bluish light pulsing with the ringtone. Not nearby. Way up the side of the hill, probably where she'd first lost her footing.

No matter how long of a branch she found, she would not be able to reach it.

Despair holding her frozen in place, propped up on her elbows, with her neck straining so she could see the pulsing light, Vanessa stared until the ringtone stopped.

She didn't want to look away, didn't want to give up on her phone. *Wait—*

Didn't she have some kind of find-my-phone app? *Yes, of course!* Sometime tonight her parents would wonder why she hadn't come home. They'd track her phone and find her.

As she turned forward, her phone chirped. The low battery sound? Would the app still work if her battery died?

With a self-pitying whimper she laid her head back and squeezed her eyes shut. Angry at herself. Why had she come out here anyway?

She'd wanted to know what caused the lights, but was it that important? She didn't want people messing around Grandpa's cemetery, disrespecting the dead buried here. But did that matter? The dead wouldn't care.

Did a person just stop existing at the moment of death? If so, why did she feel driven to help Grandpa?

The dream about Grandpa reaching for her, needing her, teased at the corners of her mind, but she refused to allow it full access. She should have visited him in his last year. He'd needed her then. He'd been family. Family took care of each other. It had been okay for him to need help.

Needy Nessa. Okay, maybe it was okay for her to need help sometimes too. She didn't need to prove herself. Didn't need to be self-sufficient. No one could do everything. Maybe that's why . . . God made families.

As the thought developed bit by bit, Vanessa opened her eyes. So now that she was stuck with no way out, did she believe in God?

Maybe she had always believed but hadn't wanted to admit it. Somehow faith in God made her feel even more needy. But she was needy. At least at this moment. Would God help her?

Branches creaked in a gust of wind.

Vanessa's breath caught. *Oh, right!* She was not alone. The lights. Strange as they appeared, they couldn't come from something supernatural. Others were responsible for them. Others were out here. She didn't need supernatural help.

Vanessa brought a hand to her mouth, ready to call for help, but then paused. *What kind of people hang out at a cemetery after dark? Psychopaths? Serial killers? Kids fancying themselves as witches and warlocks?*

No, no. It was probably a group of teens like her and her friends, out being stupid.

Not waiting for another discouraging thought, she shouted, "Hey, anybody out there?" She waited a moment, then shouted again, "I need help. I'm stuck."

Her heart thumped hard again at the thought of meeting the people responsible for the lights. And she listened for shuffling sounds or twigs snapping or voices or anything to indicate that they had heard her.

She had expected help to come from above the slope, but movement further down caught her attention.

Deeper in the woods, among the shadows, mist, and trees, was a man. His easy, strolling gate as he walked in her direction struck a chord. He tilted his head up, as if looking at her, but the distance, darkness, and mist shrouded his expression. Then he lifted one hand toward her, as if he were the one needing help.

Grandpa? Unease slid down her spine. Her body trembled. She pushed herself up on her elbows, despite the shooting pain, and tugged her stuck foot. Had to get free and get out of here!

A jolt of agony made her stop and lie back.

Not wanting to take her eyes off the man, she lifted her head enough to see him.

The mist hid him. Or else he was gone. Or maybe he'd never been there at all. Actually, what was she thinking? Of course Grandpa wasn't here. He was dead. And she didn't believe in the supernatural. So the man, if she really saw one down there, was someone else. Moving toward her. And she couldn't get away.

Helpless *Needy Nessa* had no one to save her . . .

A comforting warmth enveloped her, stopping her pathetic, fearful thoughts, stopping her body from trembling, and she no longer felt alone. She felt—without reason—safe.

A prayer sprang from her heart and her lips. "Lord God, help me." Always wanting to prove herself and feel like she needed no one, she'd not left room for faith in God. But now she realized that, yes, she did believe in something supernatural, something good, something or some*one* who cared for her, and even if she died today, she could trust that One.

No more than a minute passed when shuffling sounds

came from higher ground. Lights appeared along the rim, a whole row of them. Some white, pale blue, pale pink, yellowish, and goldish. And a guy called, "Hey, is somebody down there?"

Relief washing over her, Vanessa shouted, "Over here."

"Are you okay?"

"No, my foot's stuck. It hurts."

The teens with the lights—candles burning in colorful plastic candleholders, she now saw—proceeded cautiously down the wooded gravestone-littered hillside.

One with a flashlight slid through leaves and underbrush directly to her. He dropped onto one knee and shone the beam over her from head to foot. The light revealed his face too, and the deep concern in his kind brown eyes.

Two girls in the group discussed whether or not to call an ambulance, while the first boy and two others hefted the stone blocks off her leg. None of the teens looked familiar. Maybe they went to a different school.

The pain eased, although it didn't go away. Her leg felt swollen and thick.

"Do you think it's broken?" a redheaded girl asked her, kneeling on the damp ground in her long skirt.

"Good thing you wore combat boots," said a tough-looking girl with short blond hair and a smirk. She now controlled the flashlight and aimed it at Vanessa's foot. "Probably saved you from a broken toe or two."

The first boy and the redhead helped her to her feet. "I'm Keefe, by the way," the boy said. "What's your name?"

Needy Nessa came to mind as she struggled to stand up without crying out for pain, but she no longer felt bad about needing help. This group seemed happy to help her. "I'm Vanessa."

A guy with sandy blond hair said something about his dad coming up and how he could take her to the hospital. A girl with long hair found Vanessa's phone and flashlight. A boy who appeared to be of Mexican descent pointed out the best way to climb back up, and he said a lot of other things, talking non-stop. Keefe and the redhead offered their shoulders to Vanessa and assisted her up the slope.

While a few from the group waited with her in the parking area, others strolled with their candles through the rows of gravestones. They chanted something together, prayers maybe.

"What are they doing?" Vanessa asked Keefe. She sat leaning against the cherry tree at the edge of the parking area, her leg warm but not hurting too badly as long as she remained still.

Keefe sat beside her. He glanced at his friends, then at her, hesitating before answering. "We pray for the dead."

Vanessa made no reply, only stared, wanting him to explain himself but not wanting to ask.

"We've been gathering for the past nine days at the property that butts up to the back of the cemetery." He swung his arm out, pointing. "We hang out for a while around a big patio firepit"—the one she'd glimpsed—"and then head over here to pray."

He dipped his head and glanced at the boy with the sandy blond hair. "Someone accidentally dropped a plastic candleholder into the fire."

"Ahhh." Vanessa nodded. That explained the foul stench she had noticed upon first arriving.

"Today is All Souls' Day," Keefe added, "the last day of our novena for the souls in purgatory."

"Purgatory?" She had a vague idea what the word meant.

"Yeah, when a person dies, if they don't go directly to heaven ... or to hell," he added with a twitch of his eyebrows, "they go to purgatory. That's where souls are purified so they can be ready for heaven."

"Purified?"

"The way it's described in the Bible, and by some saints who've had visions, is like a purification through fire. It makes them ready for heaven since nothing impure can enter there."

"Oh." Vanessa didn't like to think of Grandpa suffering after death. The minister had said he was at peace now. Purification by fire didn't sound very peaceful. "And what do your prayers do for them?"

"Well, you know God always hears your prayers. So that means we can help them. He allows our prayers to shorten the Poor Souls' time of purification."

"Why do you call them poor?"

"Oh." Keefe looked thoughtful, then said, "I guess they're poor because they can't help themselves. They need us."

They need us. Grandpa's pleading eyes and reaching hand weaseled back into Vanessa's mind. In her dream he'd been climbing but going nowhere, then reaching out to her with such desperation in his eyes. Grandpa needed her.

The blond-haired boy introduced her to his dad, a local park ranger, and loaded her bike into the back of his big green truck. Keefe and the redheaded girl helped her into the passenger side. The few teens still in the parking area said goodbye, then hurried off to join their friends among the graves.

"Thank you all for helping me," she said to Keefe through the open door. "I'm so glad you heard me call out. Otherwise . . ." Not wanting to think of *otherwise*, she bit her lips together.

"Oh, you were calling out? We didn't hear you."

She smiled. "You just guessed a damsel in distress was down in the woods?"

"No, um . . ." He threw an uncomfortable glance at the cemetery, in the direction of the woods. "We thought we saw someone in the unkept section of the cemetery. Thought maybe one of our friends came out, couldn't find us, got lost."

"You saw someone?" she said, shock almost stealing her voice.

"Yeah, a guy." Keefe peered toward the woods again. "I wonder where he went. And who he was." He turned back to her. "Did you see him?"

"I . . ." She couldn't get herself to admit it out loud. But now she wondered . . . "Have you ever seen someone who died, a relative or whatever, in your dreams?"

"No. Have you?"

She opened her mouth but wasn't sure she wanted to tell him.

"Maybe he needs your prayers," Keefe said with the hint of a smile. "You're welcome to join us sometime." Then he closed the door and waved goodbye.

Yes. She knew how it felt to need help and feel alone and be unable to do anything about it. Maybe Grandpa needed her prayers. No one else in the family believed in purgatory. They all thought he was safe in the arms of Jesus. Who would pray for him? Who would help him?

If not for her.

###

Revelation 21:27 states that "nothing unclean will enter heaven." The Church teaches that God in His mercy created a place of purification for the great number of souls that die in His friendship but are still imperfect. In purgatory, "The fire will test what sort of work each one has done . . . If any man's work is burned up, he will suffer loss, though he himself will be saved, *but only as through fire*" (1 Corinthians 3:13, 15).

Saint Catherine of Siena explained that the souls in purgatory experience more joy than we could possibly experience on earth, but they also "endure pain so

intense, that no tongue is able to describe it." And Jesus revealed to St. Gertrude, "I accept with highest pleasure what is offered to Me for the poor souls, for I long inexpressibly to have near Me those for whom I paid so great a price."

With so few professing and practicing the Catholic faith, who will pray for the souls of the faithful departed? How about you?

We can help the Poor Souls with our prayers and sacrifices. The Novena for the Holy Souls by Saint Alphonsus Liguori can be prayed nine days before All Souls' Day (November 2), as the teens in the story did. Additionally, the entire month of November is dedicated to the Holy Souls in purgatory. On each day from November 1st to 8th, one can gain a plenary indulgence for the souls by visiting a cemetery and praying for them. The usual indulgence requirements apply.

ABOUT THE AUTHOR

THERESA LINDEN is the author of award-winning Catholic fiction, including the West Brothers contemporary series and the Chasing Liberty dystopian trilogy for teens, the Armor of God series for children, and supernatural thriller *Tortured Soul*, a purgatory soul story for adults. One of her great joys is to bring elements of faith to life through a story. Several of her books won awards from the Catholic Media Association. Her short stories appear in each of Catholic Teen Books' *Visible & Invisible* anthologies. Her articles and interviews can be found on various radio shows and in magazines, including *EWTN's The Good Fight*, *The National Catholic Register*, *Catholic Digest*, *Today's Catholic Teacher*, and *Catholic Mom.*

A wife, home-schooling mom, and Secular Franciscan, she resides in northeast Ohio with her family. You can learn more about her at www.TheresaLinden.com.

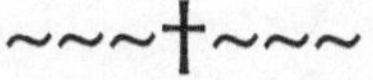

6

AT THE END OF HIS TETHER

by Marie C. Keiser

Philip set his bucket of water down, opened up a box of soap powder, and poured a mound onto the greasy metal floor next to the newly repaired crew shuttle. He'd already scraped up as much of the oil as he could. Then he pulled a stiff-bristled brush from his tool belt, dipped it in his bucket, and set to work.

He didn't mind scrubbing the landing bay deck: restoring order, removing every trace of sticky black oil, leaving the metal floor clean and dry. Making it ready for ships to land on it, people to walk on it, men to lay their tools on it.

Swish, swish, went the scrubbing brush, building up clumps of gray-streaked foam with every stroke. He'd probably need to get another bucket of water after this one, to get this floor *really* clean. He glanced across the landing bay toward the giant airlock where Uncle John and the two other crewmen stood talking. It would be nicer if they would have their discussion where he could hear and maybe even add something. But maybe they didn't want to get in his way . . . or maybe they didn't think he'd have anything to add.

He scrubbed harder. He'd wanted to be on the ship crew for as long as he could remember. His grandfather had been part of Commander Franklin's original team that had boarded the damaged *Odysseus* battlestation and realized they could salvage it. After the war had ended badly, they'd brought their families to the giant spaceship. His grandmother had stories of the first few years: trying to raise kids on board an old military spaceship; eating out-of-date Fleet rations; cutting and folding old bunk sheets into reusable diapers; repurposing office spaces, classrooms, and training areas into family apartments. And grandfather had stories too: scavenging parts from disused areas of the ship to repair air recyclers and water purifiers. Repairing the maneuvering jets with parts hand-machined out of extra hull plate.

They'd come so far since then. Philip was proud to be a part of the *Odysseus* and wanted nothing more than to make it better.

If they'd let him. He'd been wearing the ship-crew uniform and pulling a wage for eight months now. And he had no idea if he was doing a good job.

Splash. Thump. Water sloshed over the deck, soaking his pants as waves of greasy foam flowed under the crew shuttle.

"Hey, what do you think you're doing?" Mr. Juarez snapped, picking himself up and snatching up his dropped pipe wrench. "You can't leave buckets here."

"I was cleaning up an oil spill," Philip said, clamping his jaw down to keep from saying anything else. *Where else was I supposed to put the bucket? Why weren't you looking where you were going?*

Mr. Juarez glanced around at the overturned bucket, the brush, Philip's wet pants, and the still expanding puddle of water with its iridescent sheen of oil. "You're going to need a mop." He stepped around the puddle and went on.

Philip winced. Now it would take twice as long to clean up the mess. *Had* he left the bucket in the wrong place? He stood up, feeling the water drip down his pant legs and into his shoes, and headed for the nearest maintenance closet—almost one hundred meters away—to fetch a mop. At least spills were common in the landing bay—oil, hydraulic fluid, coolant—so the closets at the edges were well-stocked with cleaning supplies.

By the time Philip got the whole mess cleaned up, the bell had rung for supper. He put away his tools and trudged off to the elevator. His family's quarters were twenty levels up, and he needed to change his damp and grimy clothes.

He opened the metal door into his family's apartment and—

"Hey, Philip, what do you think?" His ten-year-old sister, Rose, shoved something pink in his face.

He pulled back, blinking. "Um . . . a flower?"

"Yes. It's a mangolia! What do you think of it?"

"It's mag*no*lia, Rose," Anne called from the next room.

Philip could practically hear her eyes rolling.

"It's pretty, I guess?" Philip eyed the paper flower. Wide pink petals, a brown stem.

"Doesn't it look just like a real one?" Rose bounced on her feet, obviously hoping for him to agree.

"How should I know? I've never seen one."

"Of course you haven't. They grow on trees. I did it from a picture." She whipped her head around, nearly slapping him in the face with her brown curls. "Hey, Anne, can you bring the book out here? I want to show Philip the picture."

"Fine."

Anne flounced into the room, holding a big book with shiny pictures. "We're making flowers for Uncle Giuseppe's grave. Rose wanted to do something exotic, so we got a book of flowers from the library." She inspected Rose's flower appraisingly, judging it with all the wisdom of her extra two years of experience. "She didn't do too badly."

Philip took the flower from her and gave it a closer look. He'd almost forgotten. Tomorrow was All Saints' Day. The day after was All Souls', when they took care of the graves. He'd hoped that this year he'd be able to bring the flowers to Uncle Giuseppe's grave himself. But he still hadn't been told if he'd be on the gravesite crew.

Which probably meant he wouldn't. He'd passed his EVA test, but the rest of the ship crew probably still thought of him as a little boy. He glanced at the picture Anne held out to him, comparing it to Rose's flower.

"That *is* pretty good," he agreed. "I bet they'll want you

on the art crew in a few years."

Rose grinned but shook her head. "Not me. I want to be a teacher."

Anne shut the book with a snap. "What we're *all* going to be is late for supper if we don't hurry."

"Right." And his pants were still wet. Philip slid past his sisters to the little room he shared with his younger brother. His parents said the room had most likely been an office when the ship had been a military vessel—and Grandpa would probably know for sure—but to Philip it had always just been home. He remembered when Mom had insisted on painting the walls. Most of the ship still had the original white paint, cracked, rusty, yellowed in spots, but she'd wanted their home to be different. She'd insisted on a "rosy cream" for the living room and mixed the paint herself. When he and Carlo had asked for green walls in their room, she'd agreed and found a way to do it.

He changed quickly and went back out to join his sisters.

Thursday was family dinner night, so they'd all sit together at one table. Maybe Dad would know who was going to bring the flowers to the graves. He'd just have to find the right way to ask.

"How was practice?" Mom and Dad both asked once they were all sitting down with food.

"Good," Carlo said around a too-big bite of rice and beans.

"I think you guys finally got the timing right on the

arrest scene," Anne said, flipping her hair behind her shoulders. Hers was straight and blond like Philip's. "And we finally finished painting the set! I can't wait for you all to see it. It's going to be so awesome!"

Philip grinned. Anne and her Tower of London. He'd seen an unfinished version a couple of days ago when they'd asked him to help them run the wires for the lights. This year's All Saints play was about Edmund Campion. Carlo was playing the spy who'd finally caught him and dragged him off to prison.

Carlo shoveled the last few bits of food into his mouth and looked up. "We've got our final dress rehearsal right after dinner. Mind if I run?"

Mom nodded, and he took off. Throughout the dining hall, other cast members were leaving as well.

Dad skewered a fresh tomato on his fork. "How was work, Philip?"

"It was fine." The landing bay crew had gotten quite a bit done, and he ... well, he'd helped. Though he wasn't sure he'd done much more today than he had when he used to tag along with Dad as a kid.

"Mom," Rose said, "Anne and I are done eating. Can we go back home and finish the mangolias? It's going to be hard to finish them with Mass and the play tomorrow."

"They're mag*no*lias," Anne hissed.

"They're pretty, whatever they're called." Mom gave Anne a quelling glance. "Sure. I guess you girls can go." The two hurriedly said Grace After Meals and brought their plates to the counter across the dining hall.

"So much for family dinner," Mom said with a bit of a sigh.

Dad grinned. "Philip's still here, anyway. And you and me. How was your day, dear?"

Mom returned his smile. "It was good. We got the shipment all packaged up and ready to go. I think they'll be flying it out the day after tomorrow. The rendezvous is on Keistle this time. I kind of wish Philip could go along for the ride. Keistle's pretty safe, and Philip's never—"

Philip looked up at that. "But, Mom, I'm on ship crew now. I was kind of wondering . . . I mean, Dad, do you know who's on the cemetery detail this year?" Usually, it was about ten guys from the ship crew.

"Juarez hasn't told me yet."

"Mr. Juarez is making the list this year?" As hard as he tried, Philip couldn't keep the disappointment out of his voice. Mr. Juarez obviously thought he was incompetent.

"Yeah. Why—Oh . . . you were hoping to be on the crew this year?"

Philip nodded, flushing.

"You only just passed your EVA test a few weeks ago. I wouldn't expect—Look, I can ask, if you want."

Philip shook his head, flushing deeper. "No. Don't bother. It's fine." The last thing he wanted was to feel like he'd only been invited on the crew as a favor to his dad.

"Cheerfully to carry the cross you shall lay upon us, and never to despair your recovery, while we have a man left to enjoy your Tyburn, or to be racked with your torments, or consumed with your prisons. The expense is reckoned, the enterprise is begun; it is of God; it cannot be withstood. So the faith was planted. So it must be restored."

Chills ran up and down Philip's spine as Edmond Campion's words echoed through the "theater," really just a disused fighter bay with chairs and work lights dragged in for the occasion. Strange that words written over a thousand years ago on Earth—a place Philip was almost sure he'd never see—could still hold such power.

Father Mousa had had those lines printed on his ordination card—Philip still had it in his prayer book—and last anyone knew, he was serving time in a Union prison for nothing more than offering Mass. And just like with Saint Edmund, the Union had found a way to call it treason.

He missed Father Mousa. And he knew his friend Tarek missed him even more; they were brothers. He bit his lip, thinking of the prayers his family said every night for the priests who risked their lives to bring people the sacraments, the poor families who had to wait so long between their visits, and for all the Christians currently suffering for the Faith.

Giving those priests a safe place to come home to. Giving families who needed it a refuge. That was what he wanted to do.

A sudden movement in the seats next to him startled him out of his thoughts.

"Excuse us," Anne whispered, waving her hand urgently for him to sit back and let her past. Behind her was a younger girl, looking pale—almost greenish—her hands clutched to her mouth.

Philip slid his seat backwards and pulled his legs out of the way. The stomach bug had been going around yet again. Anne must've offered to help the girl when she'd started feeling sick. Good for her. Hopefully they'd make it out in time.

They didn't.

Vomit splatted on the floor—at least they'd made it to the aisle—and Philip glanced up in time to catch a look of desperation in Anne's eyes.

"Just go. I'll take care of this," he whispered, getting to his feet.

Anne shoved a handkerchief at the girl and hurried her out.

Philip followed, stepping carefully around the mess. He knew just where the nearest supply cabinet was.

A few minutes later, he was back with rubber gloves, rags, hot soapy water, and sanitizer. Carlo appeared on stage wearing a poofy white collar, ready to drag Saint Edmund off to torture and death.

Philip smiled wryly. Here he was scrubbing floors again. Sure, it needed to be done. And he *had* seen the play before while he was helping set up the lights, but still . . .

"Philip." Mr. Juarez slid into the seat next to him as the actors took their last bow and retreated behind the temporary curtains.

"Yes?" Philip waited, shoulders tense. Had he

misplaced something again?

"I'd like you to be part of the cemetery crew tomorrow, if you're willing."

Philip's eyes widened. "Really? Me? Yes!"

Juarez's lips twitched with the hint of a smile. "Good. There's a meeting after dinner in the crew office to go over the details, and you'll want to go to the first Mass tomorrow morning."

"Okay." Philip nodded enthusiastically. "I'll be there. Thank you."

"Tethers," Team-leader Juarez called out.

"Check." Philip looked down at the two tethers on his belt. *Always tie down when working outside the ship. Never release your first cable before attaching your second.*

"Oxygen."

Everyone's air supply was full. All their tools were accounted for, tied on, fully charged.

"Radio check. Channel one."

Each crewman confirmed that the inter-team channel worked.

"Channel two." Channel two communicated with the support team back in the ship.

And with that, they were ready. On went the helmets, the suits were pressurized, and with one final pressure check, the nine-man team filed clumsily through the airlock's internal door.

"Tether," Juarez ordered, as the door sealed behind them.

Philip connected his tether's hook to the nearest handhold and waited for the outside door to open. For a moment, Philip could hear the clunking of boots, the rattling of tether hooks, and the hiss of escaping gas, but soon all noise faded in the vacuum. *When the door opens, the gravity generator turns off. Think of the door as up.*

This wasn't his first time outside the ship, but it was his first non-training mission. Sweat slicked his fingers inside the bulky gloves and ran down the side of his face inside the helmet.

The airlock door opened to the star-pricked blackness of space, and Philip felt his boots lift off the floor. He switched on his helmet lamp and turned away from that frightening sky toward the ship's reassuring, dull, gray hull. He followed the others along the path of handholds, their lamps casting stark black shadows as they inched their way out of the airlock and across the hull toward what had once been the battlestation's missile bay.

He'd only ever seen that part of the hull from a distance. Up close, the twisted, broken hull-plates—steel nearly a meter thick—showed how powerful the explosion must have been that destroyed the missile bay so many years ago. *The whole thing went spinning out of control, overwhelming the inertial dampeners, and making the reactor go into emergency shutdown. So much mass in motion, they couldn't right it, so they abandoned ship.* His grandfather loved telling the story of how he'd ended up on board an old Union battlestation.

Inside the wreckage was the cemetery. Open to the

vacuum, but still near the church, as Philip was told had once been the custom on the surface of planets.

On the other side of the hull, the passengers and the rest of the crew were attending the solemn Mass of the Faithful Departed, singing the age-old chants, as their gifts were brought to the graves of their loved ones.

Philip checked his belt pouch. Inside were the flowers his sisters had made for their great-uncle's grave, and other things to put on other graves.

Of course, bringing the remembrance gifts wasn't the only purpose of this expedition. All Souls' Day was also when they did routine cemetery maintenance, making sure everything was secured properly, and that there were spaces ready in case someone passed away in the coming year.

Mr. Juarez and Uncle John carried laser welding and cutting equipment because they needed more "plots." But seeing the cemetery up close for the first time, Philip thought it would make more sense to call them "berths" or "bunks."

Mr. Juarez led them in a short prayer for the dead and then gave the orders. "Philip, Javier, Finn, Milos. You take care of the remembrances first. Names are under each shelf. When you're done, join the rest of us. Don't forget to tether properly. We don't want to make the rescue team come out here."

Gently, Philip pushed off toward the nearest shelf to read the name, his tether pulling out as he floated toward it. The tether snapped taut two meters from his anchor, leaving him a few centimeters short of his goal.

Muttering to himself under his breath, he let the tether pull him slowly back to where he'd started, anchored himself with his other tether, and tried again. Gripping the edge with one gloved hand and using the gentle pull of his tether to keep him steady, he looked for the name on the shelf.

The shifting shadows cast by each headlamp formed a distracting pattern of bright light and sharply defined blackness. *Giuseppe Capello.* Hard to connect the black-wrapped lumpish shape strapped onto the shelf with the great-uncle who'd told him so many stories and taught him so many things, but at least he knew he was in the right place.

Moving slowly so as not to end up floating off in the wrong direction, he inched his way toward the clip that held previous years' mementos. He anchored himself with the second tether and examined the old flowers. Though there was nothing here to disturb them, somehow they still wore out. Interstellar radiation, his dad had explained.

He pulled the old flowers out, carefully securing them in his empty pouch, and put the new ones in, then pulled himself down his tether to reattach and do the next one.

Finally, he was done, and he turned to see what the rest of the crew were doing. Unsurprisingly, everyone else had finished placing mementos and were now working with Juarez to construct new berths.

Carefully, focusing only on his tethers and hand holds, Philip pulled himself toward them. Flashes of different colored light distracted him occasionally as the men used either the cutter or the welder.

As he joined the group, the laser welder Mr. Juarez was holding spluttered, then went out.

"What's wrong?" Uncle John's voice came over the radio.

"Laser gas." Juarez's voice sounded grim.

"Laser gas?" Uncle John repeated, sounding slightly puzzled.

"Yes," Juarez confirmed, seemingly glancing in Philip's direction, though it was hard to tell with all the confusing shadows. "You know. To counteract the effects of the vacuum. We didn't check the levels before we left."

"I see." Uncle John's voice remained perfectly level. "I guess someone will have to get some then."

"Philip." This time Juarez definitely looked at him. "Could you go get us a new laser gas canister?"

Philip licked his lips. He'd never heard of laser gas before, but he could surely ask someone on board when he got there. Going back to the airlock all by himself, under that harsh black sky . . .

"Yes, sir. Anything else?"

"No, that's everything."

Philip turned and started back across the wrecked missile bay. The path was clear, at least. Plenty of handholds in convenient places, easy to attach his hooks to. No danger that he'd float off into space.

Reaching the airlock door, he keyed the release. Nothing happened. He tried again, thinking he'd missed the switch with his clumsy gloves. But still nothing happened.

What now? Did he have to go all the way back and get someone to help him? How embarrassing to need help even to go fetch something.

Just as he was about to start back, he remembered channel two. "Hey, this is Philip, coming back to get something we forgot. I can't seem to get the airlock open."

"Let me double check on our end," a voice replied over the channel. "Hmmm. My sensors are saying the internal door is open. Give me a minute."

Philip glanced around as he waited. Next to the airlock was a bracket that looked like it had once held a rail extending aft along the hull. But now the light from his headlamp showed only pitted, dented hull plates with no visible handholds.

"Philip? We double-checked the interior door and tried opening and shutting it a few times. The seal looks good, but the sensor keeps indicating that it's open. I think the sensor is broken—we've run into this before. We'll be looking for a replacement, but in the meantime, if you need to get in, I'm afraid you'll have to go to the next airlock over."

Philip glanced across the scarred hull. The *next* one? "Where's that?" he asked, mouth dry.

"About fifty meters aft of your current location, same level."

Philip squinted, willing the light of his headlamp to extend far enough to show him the airlock entrance, but the blackness was impenetrable. Still, he knew where it was supposed to be, and there was a row of handholds trailing off in *approximately* the right direction. "Got it."

Anchor, re-anchor, detach, anchor again. And again. And again. And again, until the path ended at the squat dome of a sensor cluster. Plenty of anchor points all around, but none in the direction Philip needed to go.

In the light from his headlamp, he could see a gun turret perhaps six meters away, and a row of handholds leading toward his target airlock.

But between him and that gun turret was nothing but the featureless dull gray of the hull. Unless . . . what *was* that shadow? There was something there. Something small, too small to grab with his bulky gloves, but perhaps . . . yes, it was a ring. Something to run a cable through, or another rail like the one that should've been by the airlock. Maybe he could anchor one of his tethers to it.

A good three meters away, it almost seemed put there just to taunt him. His tethers were only two meters. But maybe, if he stretched out his arm and held the hook out as far as he could?

Carefully, he anchored himself to the handhold closest to the ring and maneuvered himself to push off with his legs. Grabbing his other hook in his right hand, he pushed off.

Too hard. The tether jerked him to a hard stop, too high off the hull for his hand to reach the ring. He waited for the tether to reel him back in, then tried again, angling his kick to slide himself across the hull.

He stretched his arm as far as he could, grasping the hook in front of him. *Yes, yes! Almost.* The hook bumped the metal ring as he slammed into the end of his cable but didn't quite catch. He'd have to try again, but at least he knew it was possible.

On his fourth try, he got the hook on.

Now he just had to go back and unhook the first tether. He pulled himself along the cable hand over hand until the second tether stopped unwinding.

No matter how much he stretched, he couldn't unclip the hook. He'd barely been able to snap the other one on, holding it by the tips of his fingers. He was several centimeters short of being able to release it. Which meant he was trapped, stuck here on the hull like a fly on flypaper until someone came along and rescued him.

But the team needed supplies. Surely there was some way to get out of this. He felt for the tools at his waist. Maybe there was something he could use to reach further and release the hook. But besides the memento pouches, all that was clipped on his belt were the—

That was it! The tethers were clipped on! He could just release it from his belt. Then at least he'd be able to move on.

Checking his oxygen levels—he still had several hours' worth—he hit the release and felt the gentle tug of his second tether pulling toward the bracket he'd attached it to.

Now he just had to get to that gun turret and its neat row of handholds.

"A little gravity would be really helpful just now," he muttered to himself as he hit the end of his tether too far away from the hull for the third time. He just needed to get his fingers wrapped around that handhold. He was sure the tether was long enough—just barely. But it was hard to reach it with nothing but that little ring to push away from.

He'd lost count of his attempts when his fingers finally closed firmly on the handhold. But now came the scary part: without a second tether, he couldn't go back and unhook. Reminding himself that the rescue pod was standing by just in case, he checked his oxygen levels one more time, tightened his grip on the handhold, and unclipped the tether from his belt.

It whipped away from him, coming to rest at the bracket. Philip gripped his handhold with both gloved hands, breathing hard.

Then, very carefully, grabbing each bar as though his grip on it was the only thing keeping him from drifting off into that black emptiness—because it was—he started down the path of handholds to the airlock.

Reaching the door, he hit the door release, panting into his radio at the same time, "I'm here."

The door slid open, and he pulled himself in and grabbed the rail with both hands.

The door slid shut and gravity returned as usual. Philip collapsed to the floor, as though his body were made of lead.

A few seconds later, the sound of rushing air told him

the chamber was nearly pressurized. He just sat there until the inner door opened.

His other uncle—Uncle Matteo—and his friend Louis helped him to his feet, unlocked his helmet, and lifted it off.

"Why didn't you tether in the airlock?" Uncle Matteo demanded. "You're always supposed to—wait, where *are* your tethers?"

"I couldn't reach far enough to release the hooks, so I had to drop them." Philip quickly described what he'd had to do to get across the hull.

"Oh. I see." Uncle Matteo raised his eyebrows and nodded. "Sounds like you were thinking on your feet. Glad you made it. Now, what was it you came back for?"

Right. The mission. Philip had forgotten everything but his relief at being back inside. "Mr. Juarez sent me to get a fresh canister of laser gas."

Uncle Matteo just stared at him. "You did all that for *laser gas?*"

Philip nodded, confused. "Yeah. He said he needed a new canister."

Louis chuckled behind him. Uncle Matteo kept staring for another few moments, then burst out laughing.

"What?" Philip demanded, looking from one to the other. "Why is that funny?"

Louis leaned against the wall, shaking with laughter now. "I remember when I got sent for laser gas. I went to the supply room first, but they told me it was a hazardous supply, so I'd have to go to the weapons room."

Uncle Matteo wiped his eyes. "And then I found you wandering around and told you that we didn't have any more, but that you could ask the crew of the supply ship that had just arrived to see if they'd brought any."

Louis nodded, chuckling again. "I think it was about two hours before I realized everyone was pulling my leg."

Philip looked from one to the other. "I don't get it."

Uncle Matteo shrugged. "It's a joke. We always send the new guy for laser gas."

"Why?"

"Because it's hilarious." Uncle Matteo chuckled again. "Trust me. It's really funny."

"So you mean they only put me on the team because they wanted to pull a joke on me?" Philip's cheeks grew hot. He'd thought he'd *earned* his place.

"No, Philip. Juarez likes a good joke, but he wouldn't bring someone along unless he thought he was up to the job. And you've certainly proved him right on that."

Philip smiled, a weight lifting off his chest. He didn't really get the joke, but at least he knew his boss thought he was up to the job.

Uncle Matteo's comm buzzed, and he walked a few steps away to answer it. When he came back a minute later, all trace of laughter was gone from his face.

"That was the bridge. We've got a problem. One of our supply ships is having mechanical difficulties, and they've requested a rendezvous. Commander Franklin is about to start preflight operations. He'll call the cemetery team back in a few minutes. The problem is that there isn't a good way for them to get back right now. What do you say, Philip? Are you up for another non-standard EVA?"

Philip licked dry lips. "What would I have to do?"

Beside the airlock door an old, faded diagram of the ship's hull marked the airlock's location. Uncle Matteo pointed to it, drawing a line with his finger. "There should be a rail connecting the airlocks together, but as you noticed, there isn't. So what you'd need to do is run a cable from here to here." He turned to Louis and rattled off a list of supplies. The younger man ran off.

"The first step will be attaching the cable to the bracket outside. We'll give you cable clamps and a crimping tool for them. And then—have you used movable handholds before?"

Philip shook his head.

Uncle Matteo looked at him for a moment, eyes measuring. "Ordinarily, I wouldn't ask you to do this— we'd have someone more experienced go. But you're the only one suited up right now, and we're low on time. The moveable handholds are pretty simple. Push the button to activate the electromagnet, and it'll stick to the hull. Push the button again, and it will release.

"You're going to use them to walk across the hull to the other airlock, with the cable spooling out behind you. Then you'll need to attach the other end of the cable and tell your team the new plan. Think you can handle all that?"

Philip nodded, glad that the heavy suit masked the trembling of his hands.

Louis returned, laden with tools. The two men attached

everything to Philip's belt, replaced his missing tethers, put his helmet back on, and sent him back out.

He attached the end of the cable, then started across the hull. The moveable handholds worked just as Uncle Matteo had described, making this trip far easier than his first had been. Securing the other end was harder, and one of his cable clamps floated away into space, but they'd given him extras, and he was already pulling himself along the handholds toward the cemetery when the first EVA-suited figure came over the edge.

He switched back to their channel.

"There you are! What took you so long?" Uncle John's voice sounded in his ear.

"Did someone tell you to get Commander Franklin's signature on your requisition form?" Juarez's voice asked.

One of the other men snorted. "That's what they made *you* do, right?"

"They did." Juarez chuckled—something Philip hadn't realized Juarez could do. "You should have seen the look on his face. I don't blame them, though. I must've been a real pain to work with back then."

As the rest of the team caught up with him, Philip turned back, pulled himself around the airlock, and clipped his tether to the cable he'd run, surprised to find himself laughing too. He *could* imagine the look on Commander Franklin's face.

"What's going on here?" Juarez's headlamp shone on the airlock release switch, then at the cable Philip had attached.

"One of the sensors went bad on the airlock. It won't open." Philip pushed off from the airlock, grinning, and let the cable guide him along the ship's hull. It was good to be part of the crew, sharing jokes, sharing the duty to take care of everyone on board, both the living—and the dead.

This story was inspired in part by Jason Craig's wonderful book, *Leaving Boyhood Behind*, in which he argues, among other things, that boys become men not by living for a certain number of years, or even by achieving a certain level of self-actualization, but by being incorporated into a community of men. And that this incorporation usually involves doing hard things, and the community involves some good-natured hazing.

Placing flowers on graves as a symbol of our prayers for the souls in purgatory is an ancient Christian custom that replaced the ancestor-worship rites of the early Greeks and Romans. It was fun imagining how All Souls' Day customs might evolve for people living in space.

The *Odysseus* battlestation also appears in *Heaven's Hunter*.

ABOUT THE AUTHOR

MARIE C. KEISER is the author of *Heaven's Hunter* and *Worth Dying For*. A former teacher, she now lives in Minnesota with her husband and young children. She is passionate about writing inspiring stories about people who struggle with Faith. When she's not doing dishes, chasing toddlers, or changing diapers, she occasionally blogs about books, life, or ideas at www.EnjoyingWomanhood.com.

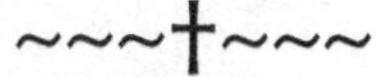

7

THE FAR END OF THE CEMETERY

by T. M. Gaouette

The frozen ground crunched beneath my oversized boots, my grimy bare feet cold and battered within, or did I simply remember it that way? The bite of a frigid October evening's chill. The bursts of my hot breath that escaped into the icy air. I instinctively pulled the rim of my worn-out flat cap lower over my forehead, but I couldn't feel the cold even if I had wanted to. Just a constant burning heat that engulfed me. But worse than that was the emptiness. A separation that was too much to bear. I was an outcast. I deserved it. I accepted it, but I hoped it would be over soon. Hoped it would be over tonight.

I slowed my speed, dodging the dull gray headstones that protruded from the ground in various shapes and sizes, barely visible in the darkness. Hanging out at an old cemetery in the middle of the night on Hallowe'en seemed a little cliché, yet, here I was again. Why?

I passed a statue of The Blessed Mother praying the

Rosary on my left, then Our Lord looking down at me from a pedestal on my right. Both marred from time but standing tall, much like the oxymoronic act of a King riding a donkey.

A line of trees enclosed the area, their skeletal branches partially naked with their fall-colored leaves spread like a blanket at the base of their trunks.

I crossed quickly over graves, taking a moment to read a few stones along the way. I'd read them all before, many, many, many times, maybe even hundreds, becoming familiar with this particular sacred ground and all those whose bodies rested here. They were like family to me.

Some worn and weathered inscriptions were difficult to read, some impossible, but I remembered them from before and saw them as if new. *Bonny Rose, Oscar,* and *Emerald.* Side-by-side, the Murphys lay, and long gone into the heavens now. Next lay *Tallulah O'Brien* the *Loving Mother and Wife.* A few extra moments' pause at another stone, *Collin Daly, 1907-1925.* That was it. Eighteen years old and no story to tell. Who'd have thought there'd be so much to pay. I'd cry if I could.

Those were the consequences of a lonely life, I guessed. Of temptations and acts of rebellion. All repented, of course, but still leaving a debt that needed repaying.

I dashed away, not wanting to lament on the sadness of that life. What did it matter now?

No more dawdling. Time was ticking away. I headed to my favorite tree on the far end of the cemetery, where the stones were newer. That's where most of the people gathered on this night. I ascended it easily, not needing to grip the knot on the trunk or pull myself up to the lowest branch. That was old school.

I moved swifter now, swifter than my former self, but while some things seemed easier, everything was still harder to bear because I hurt all over. It was a pain I'd never experienced before in my lifetime. I yearned for relief.

I found my spot at the end of a branch and waited. I was early. Always there before the others.

Would it be tonight?

An owl hooted softly somewhere behind me. Something rustled in the shrubbery below.

I scanned the area. Nothing. Must be night critters.

An orange object sitting on a stone caught my eye. A pumpkin. It jogged a memory of a time way back when I had trick-or-treated as a young boy. Dressed as a skeleton, I went begging door to door for soul cakes in return for prayers for souls in purgatory. Souls waiting to be released into heaven and eventually adorned in a splendid heavenly body. But I was a hungry skeleton. I took the cakes and forgot the prayers.

Forgot. Really? Did I ever have the intention of praying in return for the soul cakes? No, just hunger. A lonely boy without family had to survive some way. I wasn't much of a praying person back then. Prayers seemed unimportant, unless I wanted for something, of course. But the exhaustion outweighed the desire. And praying for souls? A myth that wasn't worth the effort. Prayers didn't seem important for a long time, until it was too late. At least it was for me. Little did I know. What a fool.

I prayed *now*, for those who asked.

I shot a glance in the direction of *Collin Daly*. Laid to rest in a section where only a few strangers prayed. No story. No friends. No family. No prayers. Just forgotten.

The incessant heat wrapped around me, and although I was bursting with the regret of my sins, it didn't satisfy the void. The emptiness ate at me, leaving a cavernous hole. I had noticed the feeling consuming me more in the past, and I suffered willingly, because beneath it all, beneath the feeling of intense misery, there was a sense of joy that never ceased. The Truth would eventually set me free. I just had to pay my dues. And even if it took a thousand more years, I was bound for glory. A blessed fate.

The thought triggered a feeling of delight, albeit a tiny spark. Would it be tonight?

I looked up through the branches to the bright stars above, winking in the blackening sky, as if hiding a secret.

Sounds broke through the darkness. The snapping of twigs underfoot and the rustling of leaves. I searched the grounds below until I spotted an old man in a dark coat shuffling down the path. He crossed the matted grass area, stopping in front of a gravestone. Crouching down with his back toward me, he busied himself with a task I couldn't see.

Sounds of distant voices drifted into the area. As the voices neared, their hushed tones floated upward to me.

A small group of people—a family it seemed—entered

the scene below me and made their way to another stone. Then more small groups appeared from different directions. Some individuals carried boxes. Others carried bags. And they greeted each other warmly—although in respectful voices appropriate for the setting—as if catching up with old friends. In a moment, they divided to go their own ways, to their own gravesites, where they settled their things and got to work.

One family in particular I had seen time and time again. The father grabbed withered flowers from the vase in front of the stone. Then he yanked weeds from the ground around the stone. The mother laid out a small blanket and sat on it while retrieving items from the bag.

"Can I light the candle?" a small voice asked.

"You lit it last time," a louder voice said.

The mother nodded. "It's Sissy's turn, Clara." She pulled out a black leather book. "But it's your turn to read, remember?"

More snapping and crunching and shuffling noises, mixed with the sound of muted voices, brought more people into the cemetery. It filled quickly now, and each family took their place at their loved one's stone. Families of different sizes, some with children, some without. A few even gathered farther away near Collin's stone. Were they actually praying at his stone? They all came to pray for the lost, loved, and fallen.

And then there were the others. The waiting ones. Entering the scene from all directions, skulking in, some remaining hidden in the murkiest areas of the darkness, some settling in behind trees as if obscurity were necessary. Several mingled, unafraid, with those that prayed. They were easy for me to distinguish, with their ashen appearance, dreary attire, swiftness of movement, and lightness of step. The color had been drained from their being.

Did I look like that? We were just shadows of our former selves. Barely there, but not yet gone. Essences, as it were. Transparent against the opaque world. Only we could see that.

A soft breeze stirred on my right, and a small shape swiftly took her place in the nook of the tree. She couldn't have been older than I, fashioned in what appeared to be a pale gray night dress, its length wrapping around her as she settled against the trunk. Her sunken appearance reflected her inner turmoil.

She was still waiting, hoping others were praying for her. I knew, because she was still here. As was I. And everything she felt, I felt too. We all did. All the shadows that inhabited the scene, and billions of others around the world. We were one and the same in our experience, but likely not in the cause. The only other difference would be the extent of the pain and how long we'd have to endure it. We each had our own personal price to pay.

She smiled a greeting through her pained demeanor, her grimace a clouding distortion of her essence, as if her light dimmed.

Then I glimpsed movement to each side, first on the left and then the right. Shadows quickly scaled the trees around me in the darkness. They settled above and below me. I knew more were out there than the ones I could see. I knew I was surrounded.

I was no longer afraid.

I used to be. When I'd first arrived. Afraid of the pain, afraid of the loneliness, and afraid of the strange shadows that resided in my new, albeit temporary, home. They'd moved too fast around me, whipping their transparent selves around like eels. Their eyes had drilled through me with a menacing glare. But I'd seen it all wrong. What I'd assumed was menacing, I now recognized as an immense agony that consumed them whole. No, I was no longer afraid.

I was used to it now.

A soft gasp came from the shadow in the nook of the tree to my right, and I followed her transparent glance down toward the gravestones.

A spark of light appeared by a gravestone, then another by the next stone. More lights. From one stone to the next and next . . . The warm flame of each candle sprang to life and flickered in the peaceful breeze that kissed the trees. Together they illuminated the small yard, creating an orange glow that warmed the cold cemetery.

I glanced at the shadow nearest me in the tree, and she back at me. I sensed in her hope and anticipation, as if she had a secret. A beatitude that was guaranteed. Yes, the joy shone through the pained presence . . . I recognized it in her, and it radiated from me.

She leaned down as if listening closely to the murmured

words that drifted up to us. Soft voices blended with whispered prayers.

"Does Grandma hear us, Mama?" a little voice asked. "When we pray. Does she hear?"

"Of course she does." The little girl's mother wrapped her arm around her shoulder and kissed her head. Turning to her other daughter, she said, "Are you ready to read?"

The older daughter nodded, opened the book, and searched for a page. Their father had settled next to them and now read over her shoulder.

Clearing her throat softly, she began. "For if he were not expecting that those who had fallen would rise again, it would have been super . . . super . . ."

"Su-*per*-floo-es," her father said. "It means unnecessary. Go on."

"It would have been superfluous and foolish to pray for the dead." The little girl swallowed and took a shaky breath before continuing.

All the while, my being prickled all over with hope and elation. Would it be tonight?

"But if he was looking to the splendid reward that is laid up for those who fall asleep in godliness, it was a holy and pious thought. Therefore he made atonement for the dead, that they might be delivered from their sin." She swallowed again and looked up at her father, who nodded slowly and returned her smile.

"Amen," a flutter of voices murmured from around the yard.

"If it wasn't for such a merciful God," a voice from

directly below us whispered. "I would perish without hope."

"If it wasn't for repentance," another said.

"That too."

As the whispering prayers resumed, glimmering orange ashes began to rise from the praying huddles. First slowly, in spits and spurts, but then in great numbers. They rose gracefully toward the night sky.

I was overwhelmed.

"And the smoke of the incense ..." I whispered, watching the ashes rise before us, "... with the prayers of the saints, rose before God from the hand of the angel."

Up the ashes rose into the darkness, and I imagined them penetrating the starry sky and entering the heavens.

My body cooled all over, and for a brief moment, I didn't hurt. The ache dissipated. The emptiness filled with joy. But it wasn't enough. So it didn't last long. A brief and temporary relief. A teasing taste of what was to come ... eventually.

The lapping flames returned, invisible though they were, burning with an intolerable heat that I could never get used to, along with the agony and the feeling of melancholy. Nothing could fix my anguish. Nothing but the face of God.

A gasp came from my right. The shadow glowed brighter and brighter, and she was smiling.

Is it time? her eyes seemed to plead, as if my answer would be consent. I'd never communicated with the others before. Never needed to ... until today.

I think so, I nodded, taking in every aspect of her transformation. No longer gaunt and broken, her appearance now reflected her inner bliss, emancipated from the burning agony and the empty abyss.

I'd seen it before—the change from ashen to bright colors. Her nightdress transformed from gray into blue. Her golden hair shimmered, and her eyes glistened an emerald green. I saw her now, her real self instead of her shadowy form. She was blessed with the essence of her heavenly body. She was finally purified and ready for that grand face-to-face meeting that I desperately yearned for.

Day after day. Year after year. A thousand years? Did it matter? The wait was long, the pain intense. But oh, was it worth it. So worth it. I could see that with every transformation. There would come a time when I too would no longer remember this moment, or the time before.

She covered her mouth, her brows crinkling as her eyes glistened. She glanced down at her dress and touched it and then she looked at me, shedding tears.

She opened her mouth, as if about to say something, but the sound of trumpets rang from above, seizing our focus.

I peered up, knowing what was coming.

Dark gray clouds now covered the skies, like a satin veil. The stars, still visible, twinkled behind them. Two large clouds slowly parted, like a curtain being drawn, to reveal a hue of blue that I'd never seen on this earth. Another sky, this one with white wispy clouds, pushed in around the edges of the night sky.

Then rays of sun flooded through the white clouds and into our world, shooting down like a flashlight, yet not reaching the ground.

At the entrance appeared the most magnificent sight: an assembly of angels adorned in white and glowing so bright that I could hardly see their figures. They sang with angelic tongues, a sound that broke me and healed me at the same time. They looked down and reached their arms out in welcome, waiting.

And still the whispering prayers from below filled my ears as the families continued to pray, oblivious of the wondrous event unfolding above them. And still the ashes rose into the skies and into the blue world, and I so desperately wished it was my turn.

My companion moved beside me, and passing by, she rose up to the blue sky, her long golden hair flowing behind her as if she were swimming in the air. How joyful she looked. Others joined her, purified too, rising toward the bright light above and into the rays that led to Heaven.

That would be me one day. And for a second, happy anticipation drowned the pain. I would be on my way too. I just needed more prayers.

I looked over at *Collin Daly's* grave. Still alone. Had it just been too long? Would it just be a matter of time now? If they just prayed for all of us, it would help.

Then as magnificently as it had opened, the skies slowly closed, shutting out the sunbeams and leaving us in darkness again. Dark, quiet, except for the hushed words of prayers. And then the wretched sounds of moaning from the shadows left behind.

"Mom, how much longer do we have to pray?" the little voice down below asked before sighing loudly.

"Forever," her mother responded.

"*Forever?*" she repeated, incredulously.

I smiled to myself, recognizing my former approach to prayer in this child.

"Yes, because even after Grandma makes it to heaven, there are so many other souls that need our prayers, lonely souls in purgatory that might not have anyone to pray for them. They need us. They need our prayers every day so that one day soon, they'll finally, *finally* get to be with Jesus in Heaven."

Yes, the lonely souls like me, Collin Daly.

And finally, I understood. God put me in this place every year to show me the value of prayer. To show me what I'd failed to understand during my life. The true power of prayer.

The flames engulfed me. The torment crushed me. The anguish ate at me. But joy never left me. Because even though I was still here, I too would one day be with Him in Heaven forever.

While the Church teaches that souls that have not chosen hell are purified before entering heaven, it doesn't explain much about purgatory. It teaches that it's a state of being, not a place. We won't really know purgatory until we're there, so in this story, purgatory is on earth, almost a parallel existence among the living, although not fully there. A shadow of life. Those in purgatory no longer have their bodies, but they hope yet to be purified so that they can enter heaven and then on judgment day, finally receive their heavenly body. This story emphasizes the importance of praying for souls in purgatory.

Additionally, there are saints who have had visions of purgatory or felt the pains of it, such as St. Catherine of Genoa. These saints were invariably moved, by immense pity, to pray, fast, and offer the merits of their suffering for the good of the poor souls waiting there.

ABOUT THE AUTHOR

T.M. GAOUETTE is the award-winning author of the Faith & Kung Fu series for young adults. This series won a second place Catholic Media Book Award in 2022 for Best New Religious Book series. The last book in the series, *Loving Gabriel*, also won second for Best Books for Youth (17-21). Gaouette is also the author of *The Destiny of Sunshine Ranch*, *Shadow Stalker*, and *For Eden's Sake*. The latter received an endorsement from Evangelist Alveda C. King in addition to winning a first place Catholic Press Association award in 2020 for Books for Young Adults. She also contributed to the last four Catholic Teen Books *Visible & Invisible* anthologies: *Secrets*, *Gifts*, *Treasures*, and *Ashes*. Her novels have received the Catholic Writers Guild Seal of Approval.

Born in Africa, raised in London, England, Gaouette now lives on a small farm in New England with her husband, where she homeschools their four children. When the goat, chicken, and horse chores are done, you'll find her canning home-grown produce, watching k-dramas with her family, trying to learn six languages at the same time, or writing fiction for teens and young adults. A former contributor for Project Inspired, Gaouette's desire is to instill the love of God into the hearts of her readers. Find out more at www.TMGaouette.com.

PRAYERS FOR SOULS IN PURGATORY

According to tradition, Our Lord promised St. Gertrude the Great that 1,000 souls would be released from purgatory each time she piously recited the following prayer:

Eternal Father, I offer Thee the Most Precious Blood of Thy Divine Son, Jesus, in union with the masses said throughout the world today, for all the holy souls in purgatory, for sinners everywhere, for sinners in the universal church, those in my own home and within my family. Amen.

Another good prayer for souls in purgatory:

Eternal rest grant unto them, O Lord;
And let perpetual light shine upon them.
May they rest in peace. Amen.

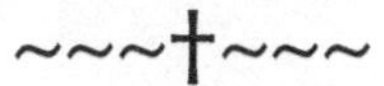

SOUL CAKES RECIPE

Prep. Time: 15 minutes, Cook Time: 15 minutes
Yield: About 2 dozen cakes

INGREDIENTS

- ¾ C butter, softened
- ¾ C brown sugar
- 2 eggs, lightly beaten
- 3 ⅓ C all-purpose flour
- 1 tsp ground cinnamon
- ¾ tsp ground nutmeg
- ¼ tsp ground cloves
- Pinch of mace
- ⅔ C raisins
- 2-5 Tbsp buttermilk

For the glaze

- ½ C confectioners sugar
- 2 Tbsp milk
- 1/4 tsp vanilla

INSTRUCTIONS

1. Preheat oven to 375° F and line baking sheet with parchment paper.
2. Cream butter and sugar. Add eggs and mix.
3. In a separate bowl, combine flour and spices.
4. Gradually add dry ingredients to wet ingredients, stirring after each addition.
5. Stir in raisins then add buttermilk as needed until dough is soft but crumbly.
6. Roll dough to 1/2" thickness and cut circles with a floured drinking glass or biscuit cutter.
7. Using the back of a butter knife, make a cross the length of the circle on each cake.
8. Bake for 15 minutes or until edges turn golden brown.
9. Combine confectioners sugar, milk, and vanilla. Stir until smooth. Brush cakes with glaze while still warm.

BOOKS FOR TEENS & YOUNG ADULTS
by THESE AUTHORS

CAROLYN ASTFALK
Rightfully Ours

T.M. GAOUETTE
Destiny of Sunshine Ranch
Freeing Tanner Rose
Saving Faith
Guarding Aaron
Loving Gabriel
For Eden's Sake
Shadow Stalker

MARIE C. KEISER
Heaven's Hunter
Worth Dying For

ANTONY B. KOLENC
Shadow in the Dark
The Haunted Cathedral
Fire of Eden
The Merchant's Curse
Murder at Penwood Manor
Penny and the Stolen Chalice

THERESA LINDEN
Roland West, Loner
Life-Changing Love
Battle For His Soul
Standing Strong
Roland West, Outcast
Fire Starters
Chasing Liberty
Testing Liberty
Fight For Liberty
Anyone But Him
Summer at West Castle

CORINNA TURNER
I Am Margaret
The Three Most Wanted
Liberation
Bane's Eyes
Margo's Diary
Elfling
Mandy Lamb and the Full Moon
Please Don't Feed the Dinosaurs!
A Truly Raptor-ous Welcome
PANIC!
Farmgirls Die in Cages
Wild Life
A Right Rex Rodeo
FEAR
A Different Kind of Camouflage
A Different Kind of Freedom
What's Done is Done
A Very Jurassic Christmas
BREACH!

Visit CatholicTeenBooks.com
for a full list of teen titles by
Corinna Turner

LESLEA WAHL
The Perfect Blindside
eXtreme Blindside
Into the Spotlight
Charting the Course
Where You Lead

MORE CTB ANTHOLOGIES
Secrets: Visible & Invisible
Gifts: Visible & Invisible
Treasures: Visible & Invisible
Ashes: Visible & Invisible

Visit CatholicTeenBooks.com for even more authors & titles.

AND SUBSCRIBE TO OUR NEWSLETTER FOR NEW TITLES *HOT OFF THE PRESS!*